Castle's Capers

The Adventures of a Naughty Puppy

By Cheryl Lynn West

Castle's Capers: The Adventures of a Naughty Puppy

ISBN: 9798656966139

Additional copies of this book are available on Amazon.com.

Dedication

This book is dedicated to my husband, Frank, who shared my love of our dogs and cats. Frank never owned a dog before he married me, a full-blown 'dog person.' He embraced this life fully, from the puppy antics, trips to dog shows, hanging out with them on the couch, and yes, handling his job as Chief Pooper Scooper. I joked that he said longer goodnights to our Samoyeds than he did to me. At least, he kissed me before going to sleep. The dogs got belly rubs. Frank would eagerly await each Castle's Capers, praising them with the endearing words "That's all right, babe" as he would scratch Castle's ears. We miss you, Frank.

I want to thank Laura Segers, White Gold Samoyeds, and Louis and Frances Thompson, Omega Samoyeds, for breeding such incredible dogs and allowing me to share my life with them.

PJ, you have worked with me on training my dogs for conformation, obedience, and just plain good manners. You are a true dog fanatic and your love and skills shine through.

And I must not forget Laura Coomes and Jason Starr for showing Castle with all his shenanigans, making him the champion he is.

(The cast of characters, four-legged and two-legged, can be found at the end of the book.)

Introduction

May 30, 2020

This is Castle. Mommy is working on the 'puter. Let me see what she is typing.

"It was a dark and stormy night. The wind howled. The Mad Author Mommy gathered the pieces of white furry posts and stitched them together. 'It's alive!'"

No, no, Mommy, don't write a horror story. People will be scared and not read it.

"Once upon a time, in a land of puppy breath and butterflies, ..."

No, Mommy, don't make it a sissy story. This is about me, not Gwennie.

"There once was a puppy named Castle, Who was really quite a hassle."

Mommy, not poetry. I'm not a foo-foo dog. This should be about my adventures, my capers.

"I told Mommy she should write a story about my life. It would be a short book right now as I am barely nine weeks old."

That's it, Mommy. Now you just sit in that chair and I will put more coffee on. I think you should call the book 'Castle's Capers.'

I love my Mommy. She stayed in front of the 'puter almost the entire night working on something called the First Draft. She didn't even say bad words when the 'puter played a nasty trick on her and hid my whole life's story. Put it back! That's important stuff she is writing.

Keep typing, Mommy. The coffee is almost ready.

The Beginning of Castle's Capers

November 4, 2016

Photograph courtesy of Laura Segers, White Gold Samoyeds.

I told Mommy she should write a book about my life. It would be a short novel as I am barely nine weeks old. But there will be more tails, oops, I mean tales, to come. After all, my name is 'White Gold's Never Ending Story.' After she finishes the book about me, she could write about Commander Sultan, The Little Princess Skye, Prince Lukie and all the other beautiful Castle Samoyeds. By the way, what is a Sucky Monster? I hear that it lives here in my new home and terrifies baby puppies. Too, too scary for me to think about.

Digging Up Sprinkler Heads

November 5, 2016

Don't tell Daddy I dug up that nasty water squirter. It's not going to blast me in the butt again.

Dancing With The Dog Stars

November 13, 2016

Mommy and I just got back from our 'Dancing With the Dog Stars.' This was my first real walk, an entire half block, but that is a long way for a little guy like me. There were lots and lots of things I had never seen before. Okay, I'm only ten weeks old and really haven't seen much. I tried to sniff everything, zigging and zagging all over the sidewalk. Mommy said I looked like I was competing on the season opener for *Dancing With The Stars*. We had the Viennese Waltz, where I managed to glide smoothly by Mommy's side, a vision of beauty and teamwork, if I say so myself. Then we did the Jitter Bug with my hip hopping around. The hoomans across the street applauded and said how energetic I was. That's good, isn't it? I added a dash of the Argentine Tango and wrapped my body around Mommy's legs, below her kneecaps.

I had fun doing the Salsa with its side steps and twirling. And I got to shake my cutie-patootie toosh. That's important. After those moves, I practiced the Quick Step. I darted through Mommy's legs, faster and faster to leap from one side to the other. Mommy was lifting her legs high in all directions as she tried not to pinch my little toes. I didn't know she could move that fast.

Mommy and I had a wardrobe malfunction as the leash somehow ended up in my mouth and Mommy had to remove it. I just wanted to take the lead. I am a boy puppy and Mommy needs to learn that I am in charge.

We arrived back home with a big finish, doing something called a Contemporary Dance. That means I got to do anything I wanted—leaps, somersaults and stretching out on the grass. And I did a pee-pee squat for good measure. That upset Mommy. I guess she wanted me to wait until I got in our front yard so Daddy could see it. Mommy ended our dancing by carrying me, her pup-ner, into the house in her arms. I think the judges should give us 10's. I might even win the Mirror Ball and chase it around the yard.

Mommy said that tomorrow Gwennie will be my Canine Pro and she will teach me to walk in sync, whatever that means. I hope Gwennie will be nice to me but I'm not sure. Loxley was shaking his head and saying I will learn Gwennie's other name.

Backyard Play

November 16, 2016

Mommy let me play in the big yard today, just her and me. The yard was filled with all types of goodies—twigs, leaves, acorns and sometimes, if Daddy didn't do a good job cleaning up, poo-poo. I like tossing the stinky bits up in the air. Mommy made weird noises, like she had a hairball caught in her throat. She was so funny, trying to catch me and yelling for me to spit the poo-poo out. She wanted to put me in the baby yard, next to the porch where I can't get away from her. Ha! Catch me if you can!

I saw magical creatures called B-I-R-D-S. They were flying around, hopping from tree to tree. Mommy said they were Mourning Doves and they made beautiful music. It sounded like they were asking my name "Who? Who?" I barked at them to let them know I was Castle, but the stupid birds kept asking the same question. "Who? Who?"

Mommy told me about evil air demons called Mockingbirds. I have to stay far, far away from them because they torture little puppies, biting us in the butt. She said they did this to my long-ago Brudder, Commander Sultan, the bravest Samoyed ever. He kept the skies around our home free of feathery air demons and even mechanical ones called helicopters, planes, shuttles, and blimps. Maybe when I grow up, I can be like Commander Sultan. Bad air demons, you stay away from our fuzzy derrieres. (I think being brave makes the girlz bat their beautiful eyelashes and fall in love, whatever that is, with us brave boyz.)

Training

November 24, 2016

I haven't been posting much as Mommy and I have been busy doing something called 'training.' So many new experiences. I officially became an Air Demon Patrol cadet, chasing birds from my backyard. Then I had to learn 'socialization.' That means walking outside and politely greeting everyone we meet. I'm good at that. At home, I got to play with Griffin, one of our katz. He was nice but then he hit me on the head. And he trashed talked me, hissing that I was a little shrimp puppy. Loxley was nicer and let me check out his big teeth. I just got little ones but they are sharp and able to tear my stuffies to shreds. And I ran off with Daddy's flip flop, even though he tried to hide them. I'm too fast for Daddy.

Today we practiced on 'Happy Legs' where I had to stand on little wooden blocks. Mommy did all the work, lifting me onto the blocks. I got treats for standing still. I like this training.

Time for a little playing and then a nap before bedtime. It has been a long day for a little guy.

Puppy Love Class

November 26, 2016

Today was a very special event in my life—the first day of puppy school. It was at Best Paw Forward. The class was called Puppy Love, taught to only the youngest puppies. Babies need extra-special loving. It is to help hoomans do a better job in raising us to be good puppies. Mommy has attended this class before with my big brudders and sissies, so she seems to understand what the teacher is saying, even if she has never mastered the clicking. That's a little box she holds in her hand to make a loud noise when I do something right. She got her finger stuck in the clicker. The other hoomans pretended to not see this, although I think a few laughed behind their bait.

I am the newest puppy in class, but I have been homeschooled. I can do my sit, stand and down, all without a cookie. At first, I thought there was a cookie in Mommy's hand, but she was faking it. I figured that out fast, but I still did everything. Never embarrass your hoomans. They get frustrated when they look dumb-dumb. I also walked besides Mommy. She looked funny, bent over, holding the cheese near my black button nose.

My classmates are a five-month-old Standard Poodle, who is graduating to Manners Plus, and a 12-week-old German Shepherd puppy named Anya. Her ears are standing upright on her head, much better than my ears are looking. Mommy says I look like I am sending Morse code with my ears flopping around and touching each other. Then there is Tessa, a beautiful 16-week-old Old English Sheepdog, who only has eyes for me. I think she has eyes for me as I can't see them. But she let me jump on her and chew her ears. I could go for an older woman. Hubba-hubba.

Once class was over, our hoomans removed our leashes and collars. RECESS!!!!! We ran and played, tumbled and barked. Then it got even better. We got to go into the big yard and play with bunches of alumni doggies, who had graduated from previous Puppy Love classes. They were all sizes, all colors, all ages. I thought all puppies were white but there is a whole different world out there. We played, splashed in the water bowl, and just had a grand time.

Mommy needs to finish typing this as I am falling asleep. She said something about a tired puppy is a good puppy. I must be the bestest puppy ever, that's how tired I am.

Recess!

December 3, 2016

I had so much fun at Puppy Love class today, that it doesn't even seem like school. Recess is still the bestest. I learned all about water, really, really, really fun stuff. Mommy said there is another type of water in my future that is a four-letter word—BATH. But I will tell you more later as I am just too exhausted to write. I hope I got an A+ today for extra effort at trying new things.

Walking with Gwennie

December 4, 2016

I have a message for First Momma Laura. Mommy took your 'fantastic' suggestion to walk me with my big Sissie Gwennie. It was great, as we both got to pull Mommy up and down the street. We are so strong. And as Mommy had to watch two of us at once, I was able to check out more things. When she was talking to Gwennie, I jumped in the neighbor's flower bed. Don't worry. I didn't hurt anything. It looked more like a weed bed and I got covered with little grass stickies. Hey, I'm a green Dalmatian.

Mommy tried to get pictures of us with her phone, but I decided to leave a calling card on another neighbor's lawn. Mommy came prepared with one of those funny bags. Then she had to tote it in her right hand. Being the little gentleman that I am, I tried to carry it for her, but she said that NO word again.

Our next-door neighbors were watching us when we headed back home. Miss Cathy must be sick because she was holding her tummy and making funny sounds. Mommy had that look on her face, like she wished the walk was all done. Then we had a special treat. Miss Cathy had little people standing next to her and they wanted to pet me and hold me. I was so happy to say hi. I gave them a billion gazillion kisses. The boy hooman rolled on the ground with me and we had so much fun. The girl hooman stroked Gwennie's fur. Gwennie looked all dignified and wouldn't pay any attention to me. Phooey on her.

I hope Mommy takes me for more walks, maybe with big Brudder, Loxley, next time. If I get tired, I can climb on his back. I'm not heavy. I'm his baby brudder.

Vet Visit

December 12, 2016

Today was another big day. I got to go to the vet's office. You know, that is the place where first they are nice and pet you on the head, then stick you in the butt with something sharp, then act all sweet again. Yeah, right. You want to feel something sharp. Check out my puppy teeth.

The doctor wanted to hear my heart. I got even and wiggled, even with Mommy holding me. When he came closer to look in my ears, I grabbed his steth-a-thingy and pulled hard on it. Mommy used that 'Leave It' word so I had to let go. Phooey. I was just beginning to have fun.

Mommy said I was growing like a weed, now 23 pounds and that I was going to Puppy Love class. I was the star pupil last week. (Don't tell anyone that I was the only puppy there.) Mommy had me show off, doing my sit, stand, down, come and leave it again, this time with food in her hand. I don't know why she hides it. I got a nose, the cutest little black button nose imaginable. I did a sit where I waited FOREVER for the treat. Mommy said it was only seconds but I can tell time and it was FOREVER. Mommy is so silly, smiling at what a good boy I was. The doctor congratulated her on my training. Hello, I'm the one doing all the work. Mommy is only my assistant.

We are back home. It's time for a puppy nap. I will play with Sissie Gwennie later. I have to keep a close eye on her as she steals all my toys. She still bops me on the head, but I think she is beginning to like me. I like her, too.

Happy Legs

December 13, 2016

I may be in trouble but truthfully, I find that hard to believe. I was helping groom Gwennie, pulling all the loose fur from her chest and face cheeks. I tried to pull some from her back cheeks but that didn't go so well.

Mommy says I have to go to rug rehab. She wasn't happy that I took her bathroom rug into the bedroom and redesigned it. Those edges were so boring and needed a puppy's touch. When she put it back, I grabbed it again and took it all the way down the hall. Then she used that horrible word 'Leave It.' Bummer!

Mommy said I needed something to 'occupy my mind.' What did she think the rug redesign was? She pulled out the Spastic Legs. She tried to put my feet on the little wooden stands but I fell off. My fuzzy paws went in four different directions, all at the same time. Hehehe. (The Little Princess Skye whispered to me in a dream to always use the word 'Hehehe' with Mommy.) I had so much fun. They should be called Happy Legs or maybe Happy Wiggly Butt, because I sure was happy. I played the 'Hokey Pokey' on them. "You put your right front foot on, you take your right front foot off. You put your back feet on, you take your back feet off. And you wiggle all about." Mommy had to act like she is winning. NOT! I am good at this game. I let her get all four feet on all four blocks and then stood real still. One thousand and one, one thousand and two, one thousand and three. Mommy started to breathe. Here comes that smile. BAMM! I fell down. Oops. Hehehe. Puppy wins!

Warrant for Castle's Arrest

December 14, 2016

This is Fuzzy Butt. Actually, this is Castle. I need an alias right now. And I need to take my lamb and do a long down. At least I think that is what I was told to do—go on the lam and lie low.

Here's the deal. Mommy just called the Castle-berry police and gave them my description—white male juvenile, 16-1/2 inches tall, 23 pounds, floppy ears, cutest black button nose. Armed and dangerous with razor sharp puppy teeth. Alleged crimes—stealing everything in sight—flip flops (again), shoes (one at a time), rugs (large kitchen rug, followed by bathroom rug), Alaskan postcards in a blue plastic bag from middle room bookcase. Those shouldn't count as she forgot she even had them. The list goes on—allegedly. She even posted a video of me, fleeing the scene through the backyard.

Gwennie won't help me. She said I deserve to be locked up. And Daddy was the rat who squealed on me. Help me! Otherwise, orange is the new white.

Bath

December 17, 2016

Something huge happened to me today. I got a B-A-T-H in the big outside bowl. First, my Sissie Gwennie got all wet. That looked like a lot of fun. Mommy must have thought that I needed to have some water play time, too. Or maybe it was because I pee-peed in my crate while Mommy and Daddy were out, and I got all stinky. It was a blast, especially having Mommy and Daddy both cleaning me up. Daddy fed me some cheese and Mommy sprayed Daddy and me with cold water. Daddy didn't like that. I loved the cheese. "Things go better with cheese."

Then Mommy put me on a really high table. Here is the scary part. A big black snake, spitting its hot breath at me, attacked me. But I was a brave little puppy. I had Mommy and Daddy there to protect me—and feed me more cheese. "Things go better with cheese."

After that, Mommy had Gwennie jump on the table. Gwennie is so graceful. She didn't need any help like I do. She stands just like a beautiful princess. All you other boy Sammies better watch yourself. Loxley and I look out for our Sissie. No messing with her or you'll have to deal with my Brudder and me.

The snake started attacking Gwennie. I wasn't taking any of that and bit the long monster in the side. It wrenched itself around in Mommy's hand and blew its fiery breath at me. I barked right back at it and it turned away. Told you I was brave. I then tried to rescue Sissie Gwennie by tugging on her tail and pulling her backwards. She didn't like that. Fine. Fight the stupid snake yourself.

Sissie and I are all pretty now. I think Gwennie is going to a big show tomorrow. It must be the swimsuit competition because Mommy said Gwennie is in bikini mode. I hope she does well and brings back a ribbon and maybe some new toys. I love my Sissie.

Ear-nition

December 23, 2016

Mommy is very happy with me today. I am not sure why. I pee-peed—twice—on the carpet and chewed the blankie in Gwennie's crate. And I dug holes in the yard and got dirty. But she is happy, like I gave her the bestest present ever. Mommy said something about "Houston. We have Ear-nition." I think she is talking about my ears and how both are standing up. Okay, the right one is cockeyed but the left one is up, up and away. Yippee, skippee! Mommy was ready to get out the foam curlers and masking tape and do horrible things to my ears. Daddy kept telling her to chill out. I'm glad as I don't need curlers stuffed in my fur. What does she think I am? One of those little Yorkies, with cutsie tiny bows between their ears? But I am still messing with Mommy. Oops, the ear just went down. Up. Down. Up. Down. Hehehe.

Big Boy Crate

December 24, 2016

I got a very special present today and all because my ears came up and mostly stayed up. You see, I had the baby crate—the itsy, bitsy baby crate. Then I grew and grew and grew. I am still growing and am big enough to wrestle with Gwennie, especially when she calls me a 'little piss pot.' Stupid girlz, always picking on us boyz.

Back to my story. Now that my ears are reaching for the moon, I can't fit in the baby crate any longer. So, I got a big boy crate. And not just any crate. This is the magical, very first ever Castle Samoyeds' crate. All the Castle Samoyed Princes and Princesses, even the Honored Sultan have set paws in this Holy Grail of Crates. The first Castle Samoyed, the gorgeous and revered Lady Alicia, graced this bed. When I am in it and lie down, I close my eyes and can hear them, telling me to be a good boy, that I am special and destined for great adventures. Okay, I hear The Little Princess Skye telling me to be a little stinker and steal the toys off the bottom rack at Petsmart. Mommy tells everyone I am just like The Little Princess Skye and she has her hands full. I guess sleeping in the mythical Castle crate is not the only tradition which I must uphold.

Oh, yes, in keeping with the Christmas tradition, I wish all of you, especially my furry cousins and friends, a very Merry Christmas. God bless us, everyone.

The Smartest Samoyed Puppy

December 26, 2016

I am the smartest Sammy puppy ever. Just ask me and I will tell you. Mommy agrees. I am so smart that Mommy must find new things to teach me. Why, yesterday I learned to climb up on the couch and Mommy got to practice the 'off' word. She pulled my fur a little, but I quickly got the idea. Of course, it is more fun if I jump onto my Sissie Gwennie's back, especially if she is chewing one of my toys. BONZAI!

I also taught Mommy to speak distinctly and slowly. She can say "Off, Leave It, and Thank You" just like a proper lady. I am so happy I give her lots of opportunities to practice. Mommy is smart, too, although not as smart as me. Daddy isn't too smart. When I try to help him, Daddy just yells "Castle, off, off, off, off. Leave it, leave it, leave it." Mommy rolls her eyes at him and gently says "Castle, Leave It" and I do. Mommy makes a funny face at Daddy and he makes a funnier face at her.

Sometimes I do things and Mommy makes a different face. She smiles, but her eyes are a little sad. Like when I picked out my favorite sleeping spot, not in the crate. It is next to the Katz' door and I play with Griffin's feet. No one taught me to do that. Mommy said that was Duncan's favorite spot and that Duncan loved to play with Griffin's feet. She said I am smart, just like Duncan was. I don't know who Duncan was, but he must have been very special to Mommy and Daddy. I hope to grow up to be as smart as Duncan. Mommy said it would be okay if I don't learn to unlock and open the sliding glass door.

Time to go exploring and see what else Mommy needs to teach me. Bye-bye.

Monsters in the Sky

December 30, 2016

Things are getting scary around our house. I think the Sucky Monster, that noisy dirt eating creature, has invited all his stinky buddies over. There were popping and crackling and booming sounds outside. Sissie Gwennie got scared and started barking. I did too. Mommy rushed in and tried to calm us down but that didn't work. Monsters are in the sky, attacking our home. Then the noises started inside, grinding and slamming right next to me. I got scared and ran from room to room, as fast as my little feet could carry me. The rugs were flying out behind me. Save me, Daddy, Mommy!

Mommy waved the magic cheesie wand. If I came to her, she let me chew on the end of it. The noise monster roared right next to me and I wanted to run away. But, but, there was the cheesie stick, the bestest thing in the whole world. I came back and Mommy gave me a little more. The nasty creature ground his teeth again, his deep voice whispering horrible things at me, but I realized that it couldn't hurt me. Not when the Mommy and the cheesie stick were there. That made the noise monsters even madder. They started screaming, louder and faster. Boom! Boom! Boom! Phooey, they don't scare me no more. I sat right there, my little chest all puffed out. Mommy stroked my handsome fur and told me how brave I was. The banging stopped and I went into the other room with Loxley and Gwennie. That stupid old noise monster. He tried one more time to scare me and made the loudest slamming noise. Ha! I came running back and sat right there in front of him. Double phooey pooey, you can't scare a brave puppy like me. Go away! Change a channel or something. Mommy was so proud of me, she gave all of us a bit of the magic cheesie wand. Yeah!

Happy New Year

January 1, 2017

Happy New Year to all the puppies and even kitties out there. The noisy sky monsters all flew to my house at midnight. There were a hundred-gazillon. Maybe more! At first it was scary, all those monsters screaming at once. But Mommy waved the magic cheesie wand. The monsters burst into bright colors all around us. Red, blue, and white. I sat so still, looking up, with my big Brudder Loxley and Sissie Gwennie. Okay, Gwennie sat on the chair with Daddy petting her, but we were all on the porch. Then Loxley and I went into the yard together and sat to watch the sky dragons light up the darkness. It was so much fun.

Loxley whispered in my ear that all boy dogs have to take part in a special tradition—the first pee-pee of the New Year. My handsome Brudder and I stood side by side, noses held high, and christened the ground. One-Missipissi, two-Missipissi, three-Missipissi.

We are off to bed now, having one last bite of the bestest ever magic cheesie wand. Oh, yes, we saw Mommy and Daddy K-I-S-S-I-N-G. Silly hoomans. They don't know how to do it right. They are supposed to lick each others' ears, like Gwennie and I do when we are kissing. Hehehe.

Happy 2017 New Year!

Puppy Revenge

January 12, 2017

Today was my day of revenge, the day I became the puppy from hell. Well, not really as how could anyone as adorable as me be that bad? Mommy has been very busy with something called the Bully-Ton, a magazine full of beautiful dogs who look like me. She has been sitting at the 'puter for days. I am so over it. Why, she hasn't even written about my undecorating the Christmas tree all by myself. "Jingle Crash Bells. Jingle Crash Bells."

I took matters into my own paws. Oh, yes, and into my own little teeth, you know, those really sharp ones. Strike #1—the living room rug. Yummy. Strike #2—Daddy's flip flops. Shake-a-shake-a. Strike #3—Dancing on patio table. She shouldn't have put Mono-pussie on the table. Strike #4—Eating pebbles in the back yard. That one had Mommy running and screaming at me to stop. I think this is really bad so maybe I won't do that again. Strike #5—Climbing—almost—onto the grooming table. Really bad move, as Mommy hog-tied me—okay, just the grooming noose around my neck and combed me whole bunches.

And last but certainly not least, Strike #6—Mommy let Sissie Gwennie and me in the big yard. We were being good doggies so Mommy turned her back to let big Brudder Loxley in from the side yard. Loxley is on injured reserve and can't play with us outside. I hurt my little foot and cried so loud.

I held it way up in the air. Boy, for a hooman with just two legs, Mommy can fly. She was scared as she found a teeny-weeny red ring snake in the yard and started imagining all types of horrible things. She squeezed my little paw and checked me over and over and over again. And gave me lots of kisses. Phooey.

I am okay now. Mommy held me in her arms. I fell asleep there. I really am adorable. And maybe that might even count for early release from Mommy's lockdowns. She calls them time outs, but I know when I have been busted. Do you think I can get early parole?

Puppy Toof Fairy

January 22, 2017

This is Caftle. I woft a toof today. Mommy found it when she thepped on it. I have a queftion for other Fam-e-yed puppief. I want to put the toof under my crate tonight. What will the Puppy Toof Fairy leave me? It better be good as this is my first toof that I woft.

Toilet Paper

February 1, 2017

My big Sissie Gwennie is the bestest. She can still be a meany and knock me to the ground. She plays and runs with me and lets me try to steal her bone. Big Brudder Loxley says no one ever wins that game with Gwennie.

Today Gwennie said it was time I was initiated into a long-standing Samoyed tradition—TOILET PAPER!!!! I see Mommy and Daddy playing with it, but we're not allowed to sniff it, much less touch it. And Mommy and Daddy don't even play with it that long. They just roll it up in a ball and throw it in the big porcelain water bowl, the one that always has a cover on it. Gwennie said we had to be very quiet. First, she told me how the sweet Princess Deirdre would gently take a corner and bring it to the puppies Rasia and Cher's noses. Then they would unroll it, while making pretty scalloped edges, like it was designed by Martha Stewart. I don't know who that is, maybe some foo-foo French Poodle.

I am a fast learner and pulled a long streamer onto the floor. Being a boy, I had to do something special, so I 'punch-chew-ate-it.' I guess I made too much noise because next thing I knew, there was Mommy giving me the stinky eye. She said the toilet paper looked like a punch card from the early 'puters. (Boy, Mommy must be old if she remembers that.) She took my beautiful creation and threw it in the porcelain water bowl. Doesn't she know that she is supposed to put my pup-child's creations on the gigantic food box in the kitchen?

Enjoying the Shower

February 1, 2017

Oh, boy, two Castle's Capers in one day. I am on a roll. This time Mommy took Loxley, Gwennie and me into her bathroom as she was getting ready to play in the waterfall. She usually puts me in my crate, but she thought I would not get into trouble for two seconds. Hehehe. Her words, not mine, so I don't have to pay attention to them. Mommy enjoys standing under the waterfall and even makes funny noises. Daddy calls it 'cats-are-wailing.' It does sound like Griffin and Jason when they get mad and smack each other in the face. Mommy doesn't smack anyone, but Loxley and Gwennie do close their eyes.

I wanted to see what the big deal was, so I snuck behind the curtain and under the waterfall. It was so much fun. "Splish, splash, I was taking a bath." Gwennie rolled her eyes. I thought I heard Loxley mumble "Is he stupid or what?" Mommy saw me and let out one of her funny screams. She even used the 'No' word. I'm going to tell PJ on you, Mommy. You are not to use that word on ever-so-cute puppies, like me.

Mommy grabbed a doggie towel to dry me. I wanted to use her towel as it is softer and fluffier and wasn't pre-coated with doggie fur. Mommy could use my towel and dry herself off with doggie fur. Then she would smell just like me.

Oh, well, bath time over. Mommy is making herself a cup of coffee. I don't know why. I give her all the stimulation she needs.

Incoming Message

February 16, 2017

I am back. Mommy and Daddy went on vacation and packed me off to puppy boot camp. It was the most wonderful holidayy for me as I got to go to PJ's in the Country, my favorite play place, for a whole week. I can't write a lot right now because Mommy says she is still recovering and is tired. (That's what happens when you get the drink package on board the big boat.) But my fans are waiting, and I will not be denied. If she doesn't let me share my capers, well, I will just whack her with my Round-2-It. Stay tune and you will hear all about Allie and Twinkle (the unedited version). Hehehe.

Castle's Vacation

February 16, 2017

I promised I would tell everyone about my vacation. Mommy is exhausted, probably from working on the 'puter and her pictures. Really, she needs to get her priorities straight. What is more important than I am? She's sleeping so I can tell you all about my puppy adventures.

Okay, here's the scoop. Mommy and Daddy sent me to PJ so I would get more socialization. I don't know what that means, but I did get to play with all my buddies from Puppy Love class. I even got to sleep with Allie. Well, I got to sleep next to her as our crates were side by side. Allie is so beautiful, with her shiny black coat and long ears and long tail and long legs. Hubba-hubba. And I learned a new game called humpy dumpy. That means I get to grab the girlz by the waist and climb on—CENSORED!!!! Okay, I really didn't do anything but someday, when my hor-moans kick in, whatever that means, this might be a fun—CENSORED!!!! Mommy, I thought you were sleeping.

When Mommy and Daddy came to get me, I pretended that I wasn't ready to go home. I wanted to show Mommy my new game, but Twinkie was the only girl who was close. Now I don't know why but Twinkle doesn't realize what a handsome boy I am. She makes the ugly face to tell me to get lost and chases me away. That is almost as much fun as the other game. Then I saw Daddy and I ran to give him kisses. Mommy looked like she was going to cry, so I ran over and gave her kisses too.

I was happy to go home, even though PJ took the bestest care of me and gave me lots of love and attention. But she is no push-over. I had to behave myself or I got time-outs. Bummer. But I know PJ loves me and calls me a cutie-pie. I love you, too, PJ.

Mommy wants her ’puter back, so I have to go now. But I will have more capers, especially as I am getting to be such a big boy.

Biker Dog

February 18, 2017

I am a bad butt dog. Why, just look at this fashion shot of me! (I can’t say that other word as Mommy would wash my mouth out with doggie soap.)

I have been bothering Mommy all morning, so she decided to ‘do something’ with me. We got to play dress up, but not that girlie stuff. I got to be a Biker, just like Daddy used to be. I am a natural at modeling. “Strike a pose. There’s nothing to it.”

Of course, Daddy had to help, whether he wanted to or not. He was Mommy’s assistant and kept the treats coming. You know we models can be temperamental, if we aren’t ‘treated’ properly. Mommy gave Daddy lots and lots of commands. She likes telling Daddy what to do. He wasn't too bad, but definitely not as good as I am. Mommy even cropped Daddy out of the picture. Sorry, Daddy, but when it comes to cuteness, I win paws down.

Mardi Gras

March 1, 2017

I decided to go to the biggest party in the world. Mardi Gras. All I can say is "Laissez les bons temps rouler!"

Terminator

March 7, 2017

Mommy is calling me the Terminator and she isn't smiling. Do you know when Mommy is mad at me, she makes the funniest faces? That makes me laugh and act sillier. Mommy has been dressing Gwennie up all foo-foo and bought lots of girlie things, like a green feather boa. She told Daddy that she was going to take photos of me, too, all dressed up. No way am I going to wear any foo-foo girlie stuff. Why, Hudson would laugh at me and Jipsi would never look my way again. No, sirree. I had to take matters into my own paws. I snuck into the bedroom and grabbed that stupid string of feathers. Then I took it into Mommy's 'puter room and just shook the feathers right off the string. It looked like a giant green Big Bird exploded. There were feathers all over the place—on the floor, her chair, even on top of the 'puter. Mommy saw what I had done and yelled so loudly, my ears hurt. I am just a delicate little puppy. Loxley tried to act all innocent and ripped the boa from my ittie-bittie teeth, like "Oh, Mommy, I will save your boa." BOOM! More feathers flew into the air. Suddenly, both Loxley and I were in our crates and Mommy was yelling at Daddy for not putting the gate up. See, it wasn't my fault. It was Daddy's fault. Go put Daddy in the crate, not poor little me. I'm a good boy, I am. And I don't wear foo-foo girlie stuff.

Mikie Management

March 10, 2017

Mommy is fussie-straighted with me today. That means she is fussing at me so I will straighten out. I can tell her that isn't happening any time soon. Mommy was fighting the Sucky Monster, wrestling with it in the living room. It was eating Sissie Gwennie and Brudder Loxley's beautiful fur. They have been shedding all over the house, decorating the rugs. I'm not old enough to shed, but someday I will help them decorate the whole house. Right now, I just write my name on the rugs.

As Mommy wrestled the Sucky Monster around, I jumped on it and bit its fat belly. Without warning, that mean old monster backed up and smacked me right in the nose. No fair. You hit a puppy! Mommy, you need to watch out for its dirty tricks.

Mommy defeated the Sucky Monster. It played dead, like an old stinky 'possum. No more noise out of the meanie weenie. Mommy ripped open its bloated belly and took out its guts. Daddy came into the living room and told Mommy how to put a new belly into the monster. She yelled at him to stop Mikie Management. I never see this Mikie creature, but he must be around here somewhere.

I reached into the Sucky Monster's belly. My little teeth are really good at pulling things, all the way across the room. Next thing I know, she twirled me around and told me to go find Daddy. Oh, well, Mommy can just handle that stupid Sucky Monster herself. I'm going to help Daddy find Mikie.

Epic Battle with Mono-pussie

March 17, 2017

Today I did mighty battle with my old foe, Mono-pussie. The green creature used to fight with Gwennie and Loxley, even losing seven of his eight legs. He is an evil, squeaking demon. Now it was my time to defend the family honor. I beat the stuffing out of that monster. Mono tried to smack me with his one stringy leg, but I was too tough for him. By the time I finished, he was nothing but limp fuzz in my jaws. I bet all the girlz are checking out my feats of daring and how I conquer a real meanie-weanie creature. Yeah, Castle, the Strong!

Hiding from a Bath

March 17, 2017

Castle here again. Mommy decided that I needed a bath today. I thought this was a good place to hide until I realized that the water hose was behind me. Bummer. Mommy just found me. "Splash, splish, I was taking a bath."

Sheep Herder Extraordinaire

March 18, 2017

We came, we saw, we kicked their woolie booger butts. Forget Sucky Monsters or Mono-Pussie. Today I took on the fiercest of all monsters—the Woolie Booger Butt Sheep. I let them know who was boss—ME—from the moment I set my brown eyes on them. Barking in my deepest voice, I told them to beware. I was coming to get them. They clumped together, looking like they had two heads, eight legs and one huge butt, just like ....

"Castle, watch what you say."

"Okay, Mommy."

I entered the ring, and they fled to the farthest corner which was kinda difficult as it was a round pen. They could not get away. When they tried to get out the green gate, I put my head next to them, literally nose to nose. Oh, they lowered their heads and stomped the ground. Big deal, stinky sheep. You back up or else. Then I took action and licked them right on the nose. Hehehe. They didn't see that coming.

I made them run around the ring again. They couldn't figure out where I would be next. Head, butt, head, butt. Left, right, left, right. I like this game.

Mommy finally made me stop. She said that I was getting tired. Hardly. Then Mommy said something that I was her 'second chance,' a very special puppy with lots of pot-tent-sell. Her eyes started to leak. I think she was talking about Duncan who crossed the Rainbow Bridge. I heard he was super special at sheep herding. I hope I can live up to his reputation. I want to make Mommy proud. Just let me at those woolie booger butts. I'll chase them all over the place.

Sheep! Again!

March 24, 2017

I had the bestest day today, although to be truthful, every day is the bestest. I got to chase woolie boogers—aka SHEEP!—again. I ran in the round pen really fast and chased them all over the place. ZOOM! ZOOM! Mommy and Uncle Louis say I had to do herding properly, not like a crazy baby puppy. I'm a big boy, six months old, so I decided to show them I knew what to do. Mommy had a funny looking stick which she kept putting in my face. Excuse me. That is sooooo rude. But I have lots of 'presence,' whatever that is. I would rather have lots of presents. Sometimes I just stood back and told them where to go. Guess what! Those stinky sheep listened to me.

After we did the small round ring, Uncle Louis told Mommy to take me in the big rectangular pen. It must have been a mile long, it was so big. I sat like a very good boy and gave those sheep my meanest "I'm coming to get you, woolie boogers." They got scared and crowded into a corner. Then I made them walk back and forth the whole length—THREE TIMES—and go around the orange cones. At the end, I pushed them all into another corner. They were hiding behind Mommy. I wouldn't let them out. Mommy told me to come to her, which I did, just like the good boy I am. After that, we left the pen. Uncle Louis said I would have earned my first HT leg. I don't need any more legs as I already have four. But Mommy looked happy and proud, so I guess having an extra leg or two is a good thing.

Oh, yes, Mommy got sheep-wrecked, knocked right on her face. KABOOM! She must have thought we were at a football game as the smallest sheep clipped her. It was so baaaaaa-d. (That's sheep joke. Hehehe)

Two Baths for the Price of One

March 28, 2017

I have a new career—Marketing. I thought it was Mark-A-Thing but Loxley explained to do that, I have to first learn to stand on three legs. I guess I am not big enough yet as I fell over when I tried that.

Back to this Marketing idea—BOGO Baths. Buy one, get one free. Mommy gave me a bath today, a mini-one as she says I have 'Ring Around the Collar' from Loxley and Gwennie sliming me. After my bath, the Blowie Monster attacked me. I love to bite its nose, especially as its breath makes my totally adorable cheeks puff out.

After Mommy finished drying me, she went into her bathroom to take a shower. I would have shared my bath with her, but Loxley said Mommy only takes a bath outside in the big cement pond and only when it is super-hot. That sounds dumb. She turned on the water and went to get something. That was when I decided to do a BOGO bath. Oh, boy, oh, boy, was it fun! I didn't just do my neck but everything from teeth to tootsies to tail. "Splish, splash, I was taking a bath." Mommy caught me and turned off the water. Bummer. I was getting ready to grab her bottle of cherry almond shampoo. It smells pretty. I bet the girlz would really like me if I dabbed some on my cute head. Mommy took me back outside. I got to play with the Blowie Monster again, this time for a long, long time. I love BOGO baths.

Castle's Poem

March 31, 2017

Castle, my puppy
Abundant happiness
Sweetest kisses
Tail curled wagging
Love shared forever
Enthusiasm for life

Pink!

April 2, 2017

I am so embarrassed. Pink! 'Nuff said.

Trading Card

April 7, 2017

Mommy finally realized that I am a real he-pup, not some Sissy-Sammy who wears pink ears. I even have my own trading card. It shows off my dynamite athletic skills, just like a Pittsburgh Steeler. I'm meaner than Mean Joe Green, faster than Lynn Swann and make more receptions than Franco Harris. Cheer for #13 on the field. (Mommy says I'm #13 because I am her 13th Samoyed. It's my lucky number.) GO, CASTLE!!!!

Dog Show Debut

April 8, 2017

This was a special day as I made my day-boot in the show ring. And while today was the big day and lots of fun, getting ready for it is not for the faint of heart. First there is 'The Bath.' This is not like any other bath. Seriously, I thought I was named after this dousing—the Never Ending Story. Yesterday, Mommy scrubbed and rubbed, then poured more shampoo all over me and rubbed and scrubbed. I swear (oops, no swearing by little boy doggies) that Mommy would wash the biscuit off the tips of my ears. Then the evil Blowie Monster attacked me. I fought back but it wouldn't be defeated. I finally pretended to be asleep and let it roar around me. Really, all that hot air. Worse, Mommy must have thought I was bad because I had to spend the rest of the day in my crate. Loxley and Gwennie weren't allowed to play with me. I might get slimed. Big deal.

This morning Daddy, Mommy and I got in the car and drove forever to Elkton, some place in the middle of nowhere where Mommy said no one would know us. I didn't understand why she didn't want anyone to see me, especially when she spent so much time grooming me yesterday. But that was Mommy's story and she is sticking to it. Once there, she tortured me with combs and brushes. Good grief, Mommy, give it a break. I'm gorgeous.

Show grounds are really neat places, lots of dogs, big ones, little ones, all colors and shapes. I thought I was in a theme park just for dogs. "Hey, I'm going to Doggie World!" But I wasn't allowed to play with any of them, not even the ones who looked like me. Instead I had to go into a ring all by myself, with this man who was staring at me. Didn't he know it is rude to stare? We went around the ring. I wanted to show the man how fast I could run, but Mommy kept saying "easy, easy." Okay, Mommy, I get the drift. Then Mommy made me stand still for the man while he tickled me from my nose to my you-know-whats. He said I was so fluffy, that Mommy could make a blanket from all my fur. He gave Mommy a nice blue ribbon and Mommy thanked him. Mommy has good manners.

Next, another boy Samoyed went in the ring and copied everything I did. I hear imitation is the sincerest form of flattery, so I wasn't upset. I got to do it first. The man gave that boy a blue ribbon too. Then we both had to come back. It was fun, running around the ring together, but Mommy wouldn't let me catch him. I had to 'behave.' Bummer. The man gave us both ribbons. My ribbon had two colors and more words, so I think it is better. Mommy smiled, told the man thank you and told me I was a good boy. She even gave me another treat. I must have done something good. Right?

After that, Mommy and I stood next to Daddy. The other boy got to go in the ring again and chase the girl Sammy around the ring. I think I will try to get the purple ribbon next time, if it means I can show off for the girlz.

Well, that was my big day-boot. Mommy just told me we get to do it again tomorrow. This dog showing stuff is fun—if you leave out the stupid bath.

Dog Show Re-Debut

April 9, 2017

If one dog show is fun, then two dog shows are twice as much fun. I must have been good yesterday because Mommy took me back to the showgrounds today. I had another fight with the Blowie Monster before we left home. I know I weakened the can of hot air because he didn't fight me as long. We bad. We bad.

Once we got to the show, Mommy bought me a brand-new collar, just for me. No more hand-me-downs, especially no pink leads like she uses in class. Embarrassing! She bought me a white one to match my gorgeous fur. Then Mommy had me trot with it around my neck. Mommy is so funny as she has trouble moving in a straight line. Sometimes I ran right in front of her, just to make her pay attention. If she doesn't watch out, she will go kaboom on her butt. We bad. We bad. Hehehe.

Mommy made me practice in the funky red sand. It felt funny on my tootsies yesterday and I did a funny little dance step in the ring. Mommy told me I had to do better today. Hey, does that make today my re-day-boot?

After a bit, Mommy and I went into the ring. I was the only boy dog today, but I still worked extra hard. I wanted to make Mommy proud of me. The judge was nice and gave Mommy two ribbons. Then I got to go back in the ring with Deja, the girl Sammy. She had a really cute butt. Hubba-hubba. I should know as I got to watch from 'behind' the whole way around the ring. I behaved and even stood tall with my head held high. The silly girl didn't even look my way. Oh, well, her loss. The judge gave us another pretty ribbon and Mommy thanked him. See, I told you Mommy has good manners.

When we got home, Daddy told me I was a good doobie traveler in the car. I don't know for sure if I was good as I slept the entire way back. Loxley and Gwennie told me not to get a big head. Then they knocked me to the ground and slimed me. Now that was fun!

Road Trip

April 12, 2017

ROAD TRIP! Mommy and I are going to a special dog show in Perry, Georgia. That is a long, long way. I even get to stay in a motel, which is a big house but you only get to sleep in one room. That doesn't make sense, but those are the rules. Daddy, Loxley and Gwennie are staying home. You should see their pouty faces. Well, Daddy doesn't have a pouty face. He said something about peace and quiet for a change.

First Momma Laura is coming with us and bringing a Samoyed hottie named Tempest. Boy, oh, boy, does she sound like a lot of fun! I even heard a rumor that there will be bunches of beautiful Samoyed girlz all over the showgrounds. I better practice my woo-wooing.

Mommy just sprung another surprise on me. I'm getting a new playmate for the trip and she isn't even a dog. Her name is Alex and she is a little hooman. Tempest, Alex and I are going to have fun, maybe even cause some mayhem and foolishness. I am loving this road trip idea.

I may not write much on the road as I will have my paws full. But I will make sure Mommy keeps a journal of all my big happenings so I can fill you in on it later. Woo-Hoo! Let's go, Mommy.

Play Appointment

April 22, 2017

Mommy says that now that she is done with the Bully-ton, she has time for Gwennie, Loxley and me. Excuse me! Since when do I need a play appointment? Is Mommy penciling me in on her Day Planner or posting me on her Outlook calendar? I give Mommy and Daddy my full attention 24/7. Mommy needs a serious barking to about her priorities. Wait! Mommy says my photo is in this Bully-ton. I guess I will give her a pass this time. But she had better get busy on my Perry dog show adventures. Boy, was I a good puppy! (Don't look at those paws crossed under my belly.)

Peach Blossom Cluster

April 22, 2017

Mommy said she would tell everyone about my adventures at the Peach Blossom Cluster in Perry, Georgia. We traveled all day to a far land where there was a magical fairground. Beautiful horses with princes and princesses on them were prancing all around. I wanted to go play with them, but Mommy and First Momma Laura said we had to set up first. We went into a huge building, bigger than anything I had ever seen before. It was filled with so many dogs, everywhere dogs, dogs and more dogs. However, they were all very stuck up, sitting on their high thrones and getting poofed. I thought it was funny until First Momma Laura turned her squinty eyes on me and yelled, “He looks like Bozo, the Clown.” All the other pooches heard her and snickered under their whiskers. Oh, I was so embarrassed. I don’t have a red nose, although my puppy hair was sticking out in all directions. Next thing I knew, First Momma Laura had her snapping scissors out. I had already seen one poor doggie named ‘Bedding Tom’ who looked like his mommy gave him a mohawk—all over his body. I closed my little eyes, quivering as the scissors went snap, snap, snap. And Mommy did nothing to save me. Maybe First Momma Laura put Mommy under a spell. You don’t think First Momma Laura is an evil queen, with that red hair of hers. Thank goodness First Momma only took a little off the sides, even if those were my cute, kinky curls. I guess I must have looked much more dapper as the girlz were giving me hubba-hubba eyes. Of course, there were a lot of other boyz there and the girlz were giving them the hubba-hubba eyes, too. Do you think girlz are fickle? I don’t have much experience except with Gwennie and sometimes she is just plain mean, biting my tail. I will try to woo-woo some of them and see if they are nice to me. Time to start flirting.

Show Time

April 23, 2017

Mommy is keeping her promise to write more about my Perry adventures. I had such a wonderful time, especially when it was 'Show Time.' Mommy worked hard to make me a handsome dude, even giving me another bath. It was okay until she got out the Purple Puppy Eater Blowie Monster. First Momma Laura brought this little square purple box where the most evil and powerful blowie monster lived inside. It was so strong it blew the curls right off my back.

There were so many beautiful Samoyeds there, my head was spinning. I hope when I grow all the way up, I can look that regal. Right now, I am all legs and ears. And I have an 'in-between' coat. Some people said I have an adorable monkey face. If I'm so cute, why do they laugh when they see me?

All I know is that this was a specialty which makes me special. In fact, I was so special, I got to go first—all by myself around the ring. Mommy and I had practiced before the show. I was ready to show everyone that I knew what to do. I was so light on my feet, I floated around the ring. If you don't believe me, just look at my photo. The judges were very impressed with me. They told Mommy what a good puppy I was. They even gave me prizes for being so special, two Lambchop stuffies.

I got to go back in the ring with the rest of the boys. Mommy put me at the back of the line. I tried to catch the others, but Mommy wouldn't let me run fast. I really don't understand how I get to be the winner if Mommy won't let me move past all the other doggies. I didn't get any more prizes. Sometimes Mommy isn't too smart. Run, Castle, Run!

I had a lot of fun in the Puppy Sweepstakes, especially as I was the only boy. I had all the girlz to myself. And I got to go to the head of the line. Those girlz loved my fuzzy butt so much, they were chasing after me. Hubba-hubba. The judge picked the older girl as her Best Puppy but I got Best of Opposite Puppy. I don't know what that means, but I got a BIG ribbon and a red-hot lead. The ribbon was pink and silver but that's okay as it is really beautiful. Mommy was so proud of me that she had the judge take a photo with me. The judge said I was a nice dog and that Mommy was going to have fun with me. Mommy better get with the program. I am already having lots of fun.

I got tired as I went into the ring SIX times and ran around. Then I had to stand still and run again. It was exciting but soon it was over. Mommy and First Momma Laura put Alex, Tempest and me in the car. I thought I closed my eyes for just a moment. The next thing I knew, I was back home with Daddy, Gwennie and Loxley. If I didn't have my ribbon and Lambchops, I would have thought it was a dream. It was so magical. I hope I get to go to Perry again. Everyone was nice. Mommy and I have a great time.

Photograph by Laura Segers, White Gold Samoyeds.

Castle versus the Dinosaur

May 4, 2017

I am getting a scary feeling that something is following me.

Puppy Match

May 6, 2017

Mommy and I are at a puppy match in a park. We are going to have so much fun. The nice lady who talked to Mommy said she should walk me around. I think they are trying to tire me out. Mommy said she is already tired. How can that be? She hasn't even started grooming me.

Oh, boy! I just saw a cutie Rottie girl puppy. Mommy, I want to make friends. I will be good. Pleeeaase!

Rumble in the Park

May 6, 2017

BUSTED!!! Big Time!!! The puppy match looked more like a Rumble in the Park. Mommy was really mad and told Daddy I didn't do one thing right. I most certainly did and will tell you about it—once I remember what that was.

There were lots and lots of puppies there. Even my buddy, Chance, the Rough and Tumble Collie, from my Puppy Love class came. I tried to stand near him so I could be there 'by Chance.' No 'Chance' of that happening. I also barked out for all the other doggies to gather around but Mommy gave me the two-fingered shush. That's where she says shush and then taps me on the nose with two fingers. The one-finger shush is just a warning which I ignore.

I was all groomed up, looking oh-so-perfect. We were heading towards the ring when I spied this little black Pommie-Ran-Here. I leaped at her and landed right on my side in the dirt and dried leaves. Mommy scolded me and told me not to play with the toy dogs. Excuse me, toy, play. What am I supposed to do with a 'toy dog?' Invite her over for tea? Oh, yes, and landing in the dirt earned me a five-minute time out on the grooming table. I tried to use the big grooming table, but Mommy grumbled that was a Picnic Table.

We finally went into the ring. I was in a class by myself so I decided to impress the judge with all my groovy moves, like whirling and racing and dancing and for extra credit 'Can't touch that—teeth and testicles.' No standing still for me. The judge still gave me two ribbons, an orange one and a pink one. (What's with the pink again? Hello, judge, you did check underneath and saw that I am a B-O-Y.) Then I got to go back in with a

Connie Corset, a Doggie Bordeaux (I thought that was the stuff Mommy drank that made her talk funny) and the cutie-pie Rottie puppy. The judge gave me a big green rosette and had me stand in line, right behind Miss Cutie-Pie. Hubba-hubba. I thought I did very well, but Mommy remarked the judge sentenced me to reform school, starting Tuesday night. It seems this dog club has a special school, just for puppies like me with 'attitude.' I asked if I could get time off for good behavior, but Mommy muttered fat chance of that happening. Hey, Chance isn't fat. He is a handsome dude like me and got plenty of ribbons, too.

We are back home. Daddy told me I had very pretty ribbons and Mommy couldn't possibly be talking about me. Time to nap and recharge my batteries. Hehehe

Dog TV

May 12, 2017

I think I found an answer for trying to be good. 'DogTV!' It's a new channel, just for doggie to watch all day. Yes, I know good little Sammie puppies should be outside, romping in the sunshine but just think how much I could improve myself. It's not like I would be playing on an X-Box or downloading videos of sexy French Poodles. (I'm not sure why I would do that but Loxley has a thing about the big white Poodles. It must be the fur cut.) This channel's programming includes 'relaxing and stimulating content as well as positive behavioral reinforcements.' Now doesn't that sound good? And it's only $10 per month, less than the cost of the rug that somehow got chewed up. It has to be better than that classical rock station Daddy listens to all the time. That radio station has been around since those dinosaurs we saw, that's how old it is, almost as old as Daddy. Even worse, Mommy sings along with it, especially the Eagles and Queen. Hey, Mommy, listen to my words "I want to fly like an eagle. I want to poop like a pigeon." Hehehe. As for that Freddie guy, he may not sound so good but Mommy is soooo much worse. She makes our ears hurt and we all start howling. Mommy thinks we are singing with her and then she sings louder. Pleeeeaaase stop! We need 'DogTV.' Maybe I can start a GoFundMe campaign. Don't worry. We won't spend any of the money on singing lessons for Mommy. I believe in miracles but not one that big.

Gwennie Is Mad

May 12, 2017

Quick! I need a place to hide—again. Gwennie is mad at me and it wasn't even my fault—kinda. You see, I'm real good at running, faster and faster. Now that Gwennie has healed from her surgery, Mommy allowed her to stroll around the big yard, instead of the baby yard. As I said, I am good at running but not so good at stopping. It's more like a bounce off the backboard. Or in this case, off Gwennie's side. I T-boned her and knocked her down into a big dirt pile. BOOM!!! She rolled and got all covered with dirt and little pieces of dead leaves. I thought it was so funny, but I guess she wasn't amused. Gwennie is such a prissy princess and does not like to be anything but sparkling white. OUCH! Don't bite my butt! Got to run faster!

New Toys

May 15, 2017

I found a new toy. It's called a lee-ver and it's on the side of Mommy's 'puter chair. She sits in the chair in the morning and reads all about her friends and what they have been doing. I tell her she should read about Hudson and Crystal and all my puppy buddies first. We need priorities in this house. Anyway, Gwennie and I were playing tug when I hit the lee-ver. I don't know what I did but all of a sudden, Mommy was sitting on the floor, still in her chair. She must have been so frightened, like she was on that ride at Disney World, the Tower of Terror where everyone drops a gazillon feet to the ground. Why, she was so scared, she screamed my name! I jumped in her lap and kissed her face which was much easier now that she was so low.

That helped to calm her for a few minutes. Mommy decided to get another cup of coffee. She said one cup is not enough once I get going. I love to steal Gwennie's blankie. I'm not allowed to have my own because "I'm still a baby in that chewing stage." Mommy puts it on top of the crate during the day, to keep it away from me. Hello, you are talking to Mr. Pogo Legs. You should have seen Mommy's face when she saw me standing on top of Gwennie's metal crate. Did you know Mommy can run fast, even with just one cup of coffee in her? She was so impressed. She vowed to send me to the circus to join the Flying Wallendas. Woo-hoo! That sounds like fun!

Why is Mommy making another pot of coffee? Maybe I can have some, to give me more energy.

Rubba Dub Dub

May 19, 2017

Mommy said "Hey, Castle, let's have fun in the tub." Seriously, Mommy, I wasn't born yesterday. Eight months ago, yes, but not yesterday. Want to hear my idea of fun?

Rubba dub dub
Just peed in the tub.
Bite at the hose,
Get water up my nose.
Spray that water head to tail,
I'm all wet, just like a whale.
Scrub and tickle my belly,
Wiggle like a bowl of jelly.
Shake shampoo all around,
Knock Mommy to the ground.
Oops, once more, back in trouble,
Sitting, blowing water bubbles.
Gently rinse those precious balls,
Hey, folks, done, that is all.

Are we having fun yet, Mommy? Hehehe

Dressing Properly

May 20, 2017

Mommy and I went to a dog show today. And this time, I wasn't the one in trouble. Okay, maybe a little but not like the 'Rumble in the Park.' No, today the judge reprimanded Mommy in the ring. Hehehe. The judge told Mommy that "she should know better than to come into the ring with dirty clothes." Mommy's face went as white as my rubba dub dub fur. Then the nice man laughed and pointed to Mommy's left pant leg. It seems I am losing my puppy coat and needed a place to store all that beautiful fur. Mommy's leg looked like the stripe on a skunk. I pulled a good one on Mommy. She didn't even realize she was 'wearing fur.' We bad. We bad.

After the judge stopped laughing, it was time for me to strut my stuff around the ring, I tried to impress the girlz with my wiggle butt, but Mommy grabbed my neck and that area near the family jewels. Careful! She growled in my ear to BEEEEEEE-HAVE. Wow, she must have taken lessons from Gwennie, as she sounded like she meant it. Okay, I was a good puppy and the judge even gave me two ribbons.

I had so much fun today and I get to do it again tomorrow. Second verse, same as the first.

Dog Show Break Through

May 21, 2017

Mommy and I had a breakthrough today, which is much better than a breakup. I was beginning to worry that Mommy would never get this dog showing stuff. She is spoiled because Gwennie and Loxley were both 'push button' dogs. I looked for my push button but all I found was a cute little belly button. Gwennie explained that being a push button dog means you are very well behaved in the ring, never doing anything wrong. I asked Loxley if that was true, but Gwennie bit my nose. OUCH! She told me not to ever question her again.

We traveled back to the dog show early this morning. First, I had to make sure Mommy was dressed properly. No fur stealing pants. Check! Extra-special bait. Check! She cut slices of ruff beef which was supposed to be Daddy's dinner. Sorry, all is fair in love and dog shows. Maybe Mommy will bring you a hot-diggity-dog leftover from the show, Daddy. Hehehe.

Mommy reminded me to be a very good dog, as if I have ever done anything wrong. (Why is my nose suddenly growing? Am I having another growth spurt?) We went into the ring and I was the bestest puppy ever. I stood still for the judge, ran around the ring at Mommy's side and stopped right in front of the judge. Then Mommy reached into her pocket for ruff beef AND cheese. "Give me some of that good stuff." The judge smiled and gave me two ribbons. Mommy told everyone that she was SO PROUD of me. "Shuck, Ma'am, it weren't nothing."

Later, I saw the most beautiful girlz dogs. Sorry, Jipsi and Tempest, but these classy white dames know how to work a hairdo. I wiggled myself silly, thinking about chasing their pom-poms. When I told Loxley, he sighed and said those gorgeous dogs were Standard Poodles. Big Brudder, there was nothing Standard about those super models. Loxley sighed again *"Sorry, Little Man, those are high maintenance divas and you are just a blue-collared working dog. They are out of your class."* Do you think if I change my collar to red to match the lead I won in Perry, that I might have a chance with Fifi and Yvette? Hubba-hubba.

I am so tired. It is time for bed and maybe a few dreams about all the girlz today. If Jipsi and Tempest don't read this, they might still play with me in Nite-Nite Land. If you see my little legs twitching, you will know we are having lots of fun.

House Rules

May 25, 2017

Mommy must be getting an 'owner complex,' thinking she is in charge in our house. Hello, Gwennie explained this pack order thing to me. She is Numero Uno and Loxley is Number Two. That means I am in third place, almost at the top. Mommy and Daddy can duke it out with the Katz, Griffin and Jason, for the bottom of the heap. At least that is what Gwennie said and I know better than to ever talk back to her. She is one mean bi… OUCH! No butt biting, Gwen.

Mommy's new rules:

1. Whizzies before lizzies. No chasing lizards until I do what I am supposed to do outside.
2. If I push the panic 'I GOT TO GO OUTSIDE' button, I must do both Missipissie and Moosiepoopsie before I can chase any lizzies. See rule #1.
3. No digging holes, especially ones with green slime at the back fence. I am not to come into the house, looking like a Comanche war horse.
4. No throwing my toys and food bowl to the back of the crate, so Mommy must crawl on her hands and knees with her big bu…
5. No making fun of Mommy when she is retrieving my toys and food bowl, and no writing about it on the Internet.

Well, we will just see who makes the rules in this house.

Castle's Rules:

1. No making fun of me when I am doing my business. No counting 1, Missipissie, 2, Moosiepoopsie.
2. No double training days—conformation and manners—in the same week. Pick one or the other unless you have really good treats.
3. No phoney baloney air rewards. No words only. I will accept real rewards only, ones to be eaten. Of course, I am a good boy. Now show me the money.
4. No more bedtime crate. I'm almost nine months old. I should sleep out at night, maybe even on the bed like Gwennie and Loxley. And if your rug is a bit more scalloped in the morning, well, you really do need decorating help. Beautiful Samoyeds deserve an exquisite and unique décor.
5. No bath marathons. Just because you cannot remember how many bottles of shampoo and conditioner you have (sixteen bottles, at the last count), that is no reason to take it out on me. Gwennie and Loxley are in total agreement on this one. If you want a challenge, go wash the Katz. I hear they are having a special on Band-aids this month.

Oh, yes, before I forget, buy more stuffies. The Round-2-Its have big holes in them and are a bit flat.

Sick As A Dog

May 30, 2017

I haven't been having any Capers lately as I have been sick—are you ready?—as a dog. Mommy is telling people some nasty bug bit me at the doggie shows. I didn't see any bugs and I know I don't have any fleabies. Mommy takes good care of me. That meanie bug must have snuck up on me when I was flirting with the Frenchie Poodles. Hubba-hubba. ACHOO!

I want to be a hot dude but not this way. I'm not allowed to go to class or anywhere else, not even for walks around the block. I have to be home schooled. That isn't really all that bad as Mommy is a softie. She grades on the cuteness curve so I always get A++.

That bug must have followed me home. Loxley and Gwennie are now sick. When Loxley sneezes, I tell him "Dog bless you." I think that is what

I am supposed to say, isn't it? People say something different to me, "Bless your heart, Castle." I think that sounds pretty but Gwennie said it is Southern for "What did you do wrong now, Castle?"

I think I should get a break, being so forlorn. Daddy said Mommy should give me get-well treats and new stuffies. I should be cuddling with something soft as I lie on the cool marble hearth. Instead, Mommy put me in solitary confinement, away from Gwennie and Loxley. Woe is me, locked in a dark room, all by myself. Okay, Mommy was there with me, feeding me ice cubes and cooling my little pads. Still, it wasn't fun being alone except that Gwennie can't bite my butt.

Speaking of butts, would someone please tell Mommy that Loxley, Gwennie and I do not have a bullseye painted on our butts? Stop with the sneak attacks from behind. Mommy is going to see a temper-tantrum if she keeps taking our temper-tures. Good thing Daddy feeds us cheese when Mommy has the temper-stick.

I'm going back to sleep now. That makes me feel better. Mommy will watch out for those nasty bugs and keep Gwennie, Loxley and me safe. I love my Mommy and my Daddy.

Personal Trainer

June 6, 2017

I am a big boy now, almost nine months old. It's time for me to get a real job. I am hereby officially Mommy's Personal Trainer! It is challenging, but I am up to the task.

My first task is to test Mommy's reflexes. This is best done when she is drinking her first cup of coffee and sitting at the 'puter. I grab a piece of equipment from my toy box, the hard ring which has been enhanced with little spikes from my chewing. Then I quietly sneak up and gently swing the prickly ring into her knee cap. BAMM!! Yep, good reflexes. She is alert and ready to start her work-out.

Next are the strength exercises. Mommy and I pull back and forth on the ring. Work those biceps. Tote that barge. Lift that bail. I am a strong puppy and could pull Mommy right off her chair, but I don't do that. Hoomans have fragile egos and won't continue to exercise if they don't think they are making progress. I let Mommy win once in a while. After that, we work on hand to eye coordination, where Mommy tosses the dumb-bone. She must use her brain and not break anything with a bad throw. I believe in a sound mind and a sound body. Repetition is required, lots of repetition, maybe ten, twenty or even thirty tosses. But you need to be careful not to let Mommy get bored. You know the saying "A bored Mommy is a bad Mommy." I vary the training by not bringing the dumb-bone back every time. Then Mommy must fetch the toy herself. She has to stand up, bend over, touch her toes and grasp the dumb-bone. Sometimes I hide it under her desk. She crawls on her hands and knees, doing push-ups to retrieve it. Aren't I the bestest personal trainer, so many ways to get Mommy fit?

Mommy is now ready for some more strenuous tasks—like the 50-yard Potty Dash. This is where I tell her we must get outside—NOW! Don't question me, lady. Move it! Move it! She can catch her breath as I do One-Missipissie, Two-Missipissie. For extra credit, she stretches those leg muscles for the Moosiepoopsi drill, searching for land mines. Points are deducted if she puts her foot in it. Pee-Yew, Mommy stinks.

Back inside for the cool-down exercises, the most important one of all. I sit quietly next to Mommy while she closes her eyes and gently massages my head and neck. Definitely a Zen moment. This helps to keep her 'puter fingers limber, so she can type more about my wonderful adventures. Plus it feels soooo soothing. I could just fall asleep. Keep exercising those fingers, Mommy.

Nine-Month Barkday

June 9, 2017

Today is my nine-month barkday. I am officially a big-boy puppy, something called a senior puppy when it comes to doggie shows. But I almost didn't get to celebrate it. Mommy threatened to make me sit-stay in the corner all day. Stupid coffee cup. I was so excited and just wanted Mommy to sing 'Happy Barkday' to me in her weird voice. She sounds funnier than I do when I try to howl. Seriously, it was an accident. My big puppy paws kinda slid forward and hit the cup. It didn't even have a Samoyed on it, so it shouldn't have been on the 'puter desk, anyway. Then the cup flipped over and the coffee splashed the first monitor—and the second monitor—and the 'puter —and the keyboard—and the lamp—and the papers on the other side of Mommy's desk—and oh, yes, the coffee splashed Mommy, too. She said very bad words. I thought about getting a bar of soap. She really needed her mouth washed out, but that probably would make her madder. She told me to sit and don't I dare move. After Mommy cleaned up her stupid old 'puter, Daddy told her to be nice to me, that I am just a puppy. And he told her it was her fault since she put the coffee cup where it might get bumped. I love my Daddy. He always takes my side and even scratches my furry butt. He also said that Mommy had to give me a cookie as I did such a beautiful sit. Take that, Mommy.

Mommy smiled and said I was growing into a handsome dude and that she couldn't stay mad at me for long. In fact, she took me out to play ball in the backyard and let me chase the lizards. And she gave me a big barkday treat. I still love you, Mommy.

Monsters

August 5, 2017

Hi, there. Long time, no talk. That is because I have been guarding our home from so many monsters. First there is the Sucky Monster. He keeps coming out and eating all of Gwennie's fur that she is leaving all over the house. Gwennie is a litter bug. OUCH! Don't bite my butt, Gwen.

Then there is the Lawn Monster. She eats all the grass and even the pretty yellow flowers. Our neighbor tries to control her, but he can barely hold on to her back. They should put the Lawn Monster in a rodeo. Ride 'em, cowboy!

Last month there were the Fire Dragons, spitting streams of colorful fire in the sky. They are beautiful to watch, but they can be sneaky, too. Some get close, just behind our fence and make big booms. Mommy yells at the neighbors for allowing these dragons in their yards. She says bad words. Bad, bad Mommy.

The worst are the T-Storm Monsters. You never know when they might attack, both day and night. The skies get black and then bolts of lightning shoot across the sky. The T-Storm monsters grumble at first and we must run for cover. Sometimes I try to stay on the porch and face the fierce wind and rain, but Mommy grabs me and drags me inside. Standing up to the T-Storm monsters makes them even meaner. They slam their tails on the ground and the earth shakes. But I'm not afraid of them (well, maybe just a little.) Gwennie is afraid and hides in her she-cave. My Brudder Loxley is one cool dude and not scared of anything. Nothing bothers him. He is my hero.

(PS - Look for another message. I got big news.)

S.T.A.R. Puppy

August 5, 2017

Castle, here again, with my big announcement. I am officially an AKC S.T.A.R. Puppy. Woo-Hoo. I have been going to school almost every week, except when I had the flu, and today I took the test. I was so good, I should be in the Paw-lympics. I'm like a Rock star with all the girl puppies trying to rub noses or even sniff my butt. Get in line, girlz. Gigi, Allie, Maggie, Corey, you go to the head of the line, so you can hear me better.

Asked Castle what he wanted to be
He said Mommy, "Can't you see
I wanna be famous, show off my sit and down
No one can say I'm a silly clown"
Mommy you can drive the car
Yes I'm gonna be a S.T.A.R.
Mommy you can drive the car
And maybe I love you

Castle told Mommy his training was good
And he said Mommy, "It's understood
Working for treats is all very fine
I can learn more, just give me some time."

Mommy you can drive the car
Yes I'm gonna be a S.T.A.R.
Mommy you can drive the car
And maybe I love you

Beep beep'm beep beep yeah

(Castle's version of The Beatles 'Drive My Car')

(The AKC S.T.A.R. Puppy program is a positive behavioral approach to puppy training. S.T.A.R. stands for ***S****ocialization,* ***T****raining,* ***A****ctivity, and a* ***R****esponsible owner.)*

Sprayer Slayer

August 6, 2017

I did battle with the Sprayer Monsters today. They hide in our backyard but sometimes, they raise their round heads from the ground and spray icy cold water all around. Mommy knows how brave I am, so she let me do battle. It was fierce, a fight to the finish. I lunged and bit at the sprayers, again and again and again. The monsters hissed and doused me down to the skin. But I finally won and chased them back into their creepy little holes. Yeah, I'm Castle, the Sprayer Slayer!

Mr. LaWayne

August 8, 2017

I am not writing about me today. And Mommy said I should let everyone know this is a Kleenex alert. Mommy and Daddy and a lot of people are very sad. When I asked Mommy why, she told me about Sammy Angels. She explained how much hoomans and their Samoyeds love each other and never want to be apart. However, sometimes that is not possible, especially when their canine companions get sick or get old. Then God speaks gently and shows these dogs the path to the Rainbow Bridge, where they become Sammy Angels who are free to run and play again. Mommy told me about Duncan and Rasia, how her and Daddy's hearts were broken into a thousand pieces, when Duncan and Rasia became Sammy Angels last August. First Momma Laura sent me to live with Mommy and Daddy. I know I can't take Duncan and Rasia's place but I helped to mend Mommy and Daddy's hearts with lots of kisses and puppy fur. They started to smile again, but every once in a while, I would see a tear in the corners of their eyes.

There have been lots of other Samoyeds joining Duncan and Rasia in this past year. One of these was Joy, who belonged to Miss Georgann and Mr. LaWayne. Joy hadn't been feeling well. Miss Georgann told her that it was okay to leave her sister Kona, and brothers Pepper and Tuch-ka. God welcomed Joy but He could tell that she was missing her Mommy and Daddy. He looked down and saw that Mr. LaWayne was not feeling well, just like Joy had been sick. God watches over all of us and He knew that Mr. LaWayne was a special person, kind and gentle, and that Mr. LaWayne loved all Samoyeds and even other animals too. God whispered in Mr. LaWayne's ear, asking if he would like to cross the Rainbow Bridge. Mr. LaWayne would become a special Sammy Angel—a human one—to play with the animals there. He could even do some herding with a heavenly crook, made especially by God, which sparkled in the sun. Mr. LaWayne knew his family and friends would be sad, but he understood God needed him. The only thing he asked of God was for Him to continue to watch over his wife, Miss Georgann and his two beautiful daughters, CJ and Denise. God promised he would lovingly do that.

So, if you see the clouds blowing gently across the sky, squint your eyes just a little and maybe you will see Mr. LaWayne and Joy, herding those sheep clouds around Heaven.

Trick Dog

August 20, 2017

I haven't been writing much lately as I have been practicing for my big test. It was actually two tests and I aced both of them. Okay, maybe I wasn't as good as all of the Flat Coated Retrievers but I think they had a study group. But I did good enough to get two—yes, two, not one—titles. I am going to have bunches of letters behind my name. At first, I thought I had to drag them behind my butt and that could get hard. Mommy says I need titles at both ends. Gee, isn't being the most adorable hubba-hubba Samoyed puppy enough? I guess Mommy has big plans for me.

Back to my titles. I am now an AKC Trick Dog Novice and Do More With Your Dog Novice Trick Dog. I had to do ten tricks for the AKC title and 15 for the DMWYD title. Some tricks were easy, like kissing Mommy on her face. I think I should have gotten extra credit as I gave her a big sloppy kiss right on the lips. Hehehe. Others took more talents, like rolling over and crawling on my belly for five feet. And I had to do everything twice, just to prove I could really do each trick. It was a lot of fun. Gigi, my Golden Retriever cutie-pie crush, was there to see how well I performed. I was willing to do a back flip for her.

Gwennie is not being nice to me right now. She said that the circus is looking for Bozo the Clown Dog and maybe I should run away and join the circus. She's a poor sport as she didn't pass her Canine Good Citizen. Gwennie couldn't keep her fat bottom butt in one place and didn't do her sit-stay. QUCH! Gwennie, don't bite my butt. Loxley didn't pass either, but he is not a meanie. He said he just needed a little more practice as he has been on injured reserve. Gwennie jumped on him and hurt his back leg. See, I told you she was a meannie. Don't bite me, Gwennie.

I'm going to close my eyes for just a little while. Maybe I will dream of the medals I will win at the Paw-lympics.

Cheap Shot

August 29, 2017

Gwennie is in big trouble! And Mommy and Daddy aren't happy. She is such a meanie and picks on both Loxley and me but she picks more on me. She thinks my butt is a squeaky toy. OUCH! Today she took a cheap shot at me as we were going outside. I jumped backwards—right into the pool screen door. I hit it so hard, the metal plate on the bottom popped right out of the groove. Mommy tried to fix it with a big hammer and duck tape. Why would Mommy want to tape a duck? Wouldn't that hurt the duck's butt? Maybe she is not as good as she is quacked up to be. Now they need to find a repair person to fix the door. I hope they ground Gwennie and take the cost out of her treat allowance. Loxley and I will be glad to eat her share. And she needs to kiss my cute little butt and make it feel better. OUCH! That's not a kiss, Gwennie.

Castle's First Barkday

September 8, 2017

Tomorrow is a very big day for me. It is my first barkday. I thought I was just going to my Saturday Manners Plus class and then Puppy Play time with all my puppy buds. But for some reason, my teacher PJ isn't having any classes in Osteen. Then I got to thinking that Mommy was planning a special surprise paw-tie for me. She must have invited all my friends as she has been bringing the chairs and tables from the porch into the house. There will be a nice big soft chaise lounge for Gigi and another for Corey and one for Bailey and an extra special one for Allie.

Loxley mentioned something about this could be a Hurry Cane party. Do Hurry Canes taste like Candy Canes? If they do, I will lick each one and then give sticky kisses to all my girlfriends. Hubba-hubba. And Loxley said the house would be all lit up with candles, not just one. I get to blow them all out.

Gwennie said I shouldn't have a paw-ty because I am not a real man doggie yet. She is so mean. She makes fun of me because I can't figure out how to stand on three legs like Loxley does when I do my Missipissiee. She shouldn't tell anyone about that. The other boy doggies will laugh at me. Just for that, I am not going to sniff her oh-so-precious butt and I am certainly not going to give her any sticky Hurry Cane kisses.

See you at the paw-tie on Saturday. Happy Barkday to me. Happy Barkday, Dear Castle. Happy Barkday to me.

Love My Octopussie

October 31, 2017

Loxley with the new Octopussie

I love, love, love my Octopussie! Even my Brudder Loxley loves my Octopussie.

New BFF

November 19, 2017

I apologize for Mommy's lack of attention to my adventures. But I guess I'm stuck with her. Daddy doesn't do Facebook. Gwennie said she would do it, but I don't trust her. I saw her working on something called Gwen's Glam Tips.

Speaking about good stuff, I went to a bunch of shows in Ocala this weekend. And now I have a new BFF Laura. She's pretty and runs around the ring with me. I like her and always behave like a perfect gentleman. Gwennie is jealous as Laura used to be her BFF. Haha, Gwennie, Laura likes me bestest.

I got lots of ribbons, a different color each day. Mommy didn't seem happy with some of them, but she said the competition is crazy good. She was happy for her friends who got lots of pretty ribbons, too.

Today I got two ribbons. The first time Laura and I ran around the ring, I got a blue ribbon. The next time I got a purple ribbon. Mommy started to act all weird outside the ring, jumping up and down and punching Mr. Louis on the shoulder. And she was making little squeaking sounds. Mommy, you're so funny.

Miss Laura was so proud of me. She told the judge she wanted a picture of the three of us. She even had the picture taker put special words on the sign—Major Win and Winner Dog. I had to stand still and look hubba-hubba. I think I will send paw-tograph copies to all my girlfriends.

Bedroom Privileges

November 21, 2017

I am a really big boy now. I got bedroom privileges. That is a super big deal because it means Mommy and Daddy trust me when they have their eyes closed. I don't have to sleep in my metal box bed. I still curl up in it but now Mommy leaves the door open. You see, Loxley and Gwennie already have the best spots. Loxley sleeps in the shower, with the curtain drawn and Gwennie sleeps on the bed between Mommy and Daddy.

This morning, after Gwennie got off the bed, I decided it was my turn, snuggling next to Mommy and Daddy. I jumped on the bed before Loxley could get up there. That bed is so soft and warm, I just wanted to wiggle until I found the perfect spot. Mommy growled at me. "Go lie down."

I love Mommy so much, I wanted to give her a big kiss but she sleeps with a gentle leader on her face, with a muzzle on her nose, straps around her head and a long round leash attached to a box. Do I look that funny when I have my gentle leader on? I decided to kiss her toes instead and nibble on her foot. Mommy must have liked that because she took the gentle leader off her face and took us outside to play.

Bedroom privileges are so much fun. I can't wait to see what I can do tonight.

Christmas Photos

November 25, 2017

Mommy and I had so much fun today. We went to class at Best Paw Forward, but I didn't have to do any of that obedience stuff. Instead, Mommy brought her camera and took lots of Christmas pictures. This is a BIG PRODUCTION as these are special photos. Mommy got on the ground, Miss PJ hid behind the backdrop to hold the puppy leashes and the rest of the people stood behind Mommy making funny sounds. Hoomans are so silly. Don't they know we are naturally beautiful? "Strike a pose. There's nothing to it."

I was a good boy and waited patiently for my turn. I let all my girlfriends and the new puppies go first. Allie, Maggie and Corey looked so sweet. Even Twinkle look pretty in her red sweater. I didn't go too close to her as she doesn’t like me. Maybe I shouldn’t have stuck my nose somewhere it didn’t belong. It was finally my turn. Mommy was busy, focusing on my beautiful brown eyes, that she didn’t notice I did something bad. And I would have gotten away with it if Miss PJ and Miss Karen didn’t snitch on me. I colored the snow mat. Hey, Mommy, don’t eat the yellow snow. Hehehe.

Mommy is now working on the pictures and will post them soon. I told her I wanted my gorgeous mug posted first. Then maybe Santa Paws will see it and think I have been a good boy, well, mostly. I’m a little good behavior challenged. If that doesn’t work, I will put my profile on HandsomeHunk.dog. Anyone got any mistletoe?

Orlando Dog Show

December 14, 2017

I had a fun day yesterday. I got to go to the super big dog show in Orlando. There were thousands of dogs, some that I had never seen before. Mommy acts like she knows all their names. “Oh, is this a Hungarian Wirehaired Wienerschnitzel?” “That's a Kookie Hound.” “Check out the Show Me.” Show me what, Mommy? All I see are dogs.

We walked past the Standard White Poodles. Be still, my beating heart. Those are some real classy dames, with their fancy pom-poms and long, slender legs. Hubba, hubba. They stuck their noses in the air, ignoring me. I guess I’m not good enough, being just a young working dog. But a guy can dream, can’t he? Or maybe I should just stick with my sweet Sammie girlfriends. They know how to have a good time and not worry about their poofie fur getting all frizzie.

Later, I got to be a ‘demo’ dog. At first, I thought that meant demolition dog and I was ready to rumble with the other dogs. Imagine my surprise when I had to be good—really good, like show ring good. Mommy and I did something called judges’ education. Mommy made me stand still while she waved some roast beef in my face. Well, I have been doing some education myself and I knew not to do the happy feet dance. Let me tell you, Mommy needs to up her game and give me bigger pieces. She is STINGY. Hey, a dog could starve on the itsy-bitsy pieces she doles out. I liked when the other lady held me. I got the whole big piece in one bite. Hehehe. After that, all the people came around and started to pet me on the head, down to my cute derriere. Maybe they just needed a Sammie fix.

After we were done, Mommy had to interview several of the nice ladies who talked earlier. I wanted to play with the cute Sammy girl, next to me. Hey, want to check out my Jingle Balls? One of the ladies took my leash and said she would hold me. She explained that she was used to young boyz. Let’s just say I decided to behave. In fact, I decided to be good for the rest of the day, even when we walked back to the grooming area. I hope Mommy appreciated that because that was her Christmas present, as if she deserved anything for her stingy, stingy treats.

Merry Christmas, everyone. Fleas Naughty Dogs.

Naughty or Nice List

December 23, 2017

I need some help understanding this Christmas thing. Gwennie explained it to me but I don't trust her. After all, she is a girl and Loxley said to never trust girlz, especially Sammy girlz. He didn't say why but my big brudder is one smart dude. Gwennie said Santa Paws has a Naughty or Nice List. It is a long, long list which tells Santa Paws what you did during the year. I don't know why he needs to write it down. I remember every moment perfectly—and I do mean perfectly as I was perfect. Gwennie said that just showed what a dumb puppy I am. She then showed me Santa Paws' list.

Nice:

Guinevere, the Beautiful - Absolutely good
Loxley - Laid back good
Griffin and Jason - Good, considering they are Katz

Naughty:

Castle - Let me count the ways.
Castle - Destroyed all the stuffie toys, including the Mono-Pussie
Castle - Dug holes so deep Mommy had to fill them with poop
Castle - Held back in Manners class
Castle - Chased the other Sammies in the show ring
Castle - Etc., etc., etc. Shall we go on?

As if that stupid list isn't bad enough, I saw Gwennie messing with our presents. I wasn't really trying to find out where Mommy hid them. I was—let me see—oh, yes, I was just trying to make sure Mommy had enough wrapping paper for all my presents. Gwennie had a pencil and was putting big X's through my name and printing 'G-W-E-N.' What does that mean? She told me to go get the largest stocking and put my name on it, so it can hold all the coal Santa Paws is bringing me. After that, she sang my personal Christmas song 'Fleas Naughty Dog.'

I am going to stay up late and have a talk with Santa Paws when he wiggles down our chimney. I might even save him a cookie from the plate which Mommy sets out on Christmas Eve.

Merry Christmas, everyone, from the Truly Good Castle. (Just ask anyone, except Gwennie.)

Three Strikes

December 28, 2017

It's a good thing Santa Paws can't take back Christmas presents. If he did, I would not have any. Wait, Gwennie took all my presents, so I don't have any. Bummer.

I had a little trouble being good today. Well, maybe I had a lot of trouble. It started when I tried to wake Mommy up. She was sleeping with that crappy mask on her face. At least, she doesn't snore now, which makes us all happy, especially Daddy. I jumped up to kiss her, like Prince Charming woke up Sleeping Beauty. It wasn't my fault that my leg got tangled with the hose attached to her nose. She fell out of the bed, right on her head. KABOOM! Strike One!

Then I got to run in the big yard, now that the bees are gone from the tree and the fence is back in place. Mommy was having so much fun, filling in a hole. I decided to make her even happier. When she turned her back, I power dug the biggest, deepest hole in the whole world. And I hid the dirt. (It's a secret where I hid it. I will tell you later.) She came running across the yard, waving the pooper scooper at me. I thought we were having a good time, but Mommy said some bad words. I think that means I was bad—again. Strike Two.

Later, Loxley and I were in the kitchen when we spied the Scary-Moochie Katz in our yard. Excuse me, buster, scat! That stupid katz leaped on the fence, sneered at us and licked his private parts, if you know what I mean. Gross. Loxley and I lunged at the window, barking in our most furious voices. The plastic white pieces hanging on the window clattered and swung around, almost coming down on top of brave Loxley and me. And that stupid katz just kept licking and licking. Mommy had to go outside and make that hideous monster leave. I don't know why Daddy feeds it. Then Mommy came in and yelled at me. WHAT?! Didn't you see I was protecting Castle's castle? None of the plastic pieces were broken—this time. Oops, Strike Three and I am in the metal bedroom.

After dinner, Mommy and Daddy took me to the vet's office. I got on the scale and showed them that I didn't gain weight from eating too many Christmas cookies, not like someone I know. I sat in the waiting room, like such a perfect gentleman, not the evil puppy Mommy tries to tell everyone that I am. Take that, Mommy, no one believes you. Hehehe. But that didn't save me from Mommy's evil scheme. She let the doctor give me not one, not two but three shots, all in my cute little derriere, one for each strike. I took it like a true Sammy big boy, not a whimper. Mommy thought that made us even. Then I really embarrassed her. The doctor checked my heart and tonsils and finally my ears. Surprise, Mommy! The doctor found where I hid all the dirt from the hole. He laughed at Mommy's red face and said, yep, that looks like Casselberry dirt. Paybacks are hell, Mommy.

Look Up

March 14, 2018

For those who don't know, I am the most adorable Samoyed puppy. Now some of you seeing me can't believe that. Not that I am the most beautiful, fuzzy, white fur ball in the entire universe, but that I am still a puppy. I'm now a big boy puppy, sixty-two pounds and 18 months old. But last year, I was just a little squirt.

That was when I learned the importance of 'Look Up.' I had to do that to survive. Everything was above me. Well, almost everything. Griffin and Jason, the sneaky-peeky katz, were the same size as I was. But they jumped on the chairs and hid under the table. Then they would take nasty swipes at my cute little butt with their evil claws. It was 'Look Up and Look Out' for them.

Loxley is my big brudder. I was so short that I could run clean under his belly back then. He is a boy doggie so if I didn't look up, I would run into his 'thingie.' Pee-Yew. Look Up!

Mommy took me to Puppy Love class every Saturday. That is the bestest place to learn 'Look Up.' Mommy would have delicious goodies in her hand. All I had to do was to Look Up and she would give me cheese and even a teeny weenie bit of French fries. Sometimes Mommy would wiggle her hands around in the air and I would sit or stand or lay down. I didn't always get it right, but Miss PJ made Mommy pay if I made an effort to Look Up.

At bedtime, Mommy and Daddy would climb way up high to sleep on the soft bed. I wasn't allowed 'bedroom privileges' as I still wee-wee'd on the rug. Mommy would kiss me and put me in my special crib. I could Look Up and see them. I knew I was safe and loved. I would also see my bratty Sissie Gwennie, looking down on me. Just you wait, Gwennie. Someday I will be big, and you will Look Up at me. OUCH! I didn't mean that, Gwennie. I will always Look Up to you.

Pet Exposé

March 22, 2018

My Mommy went to a Pet Exposé. At least, that is what I think it was called. Mommy went to investigate new dog foods, herbal medicines and even poopie bags. It was in a huge building with people from all over the country, Canada and even from China. I don't know why Mommy didn't take me. Put a trench coat and a pair of sunglasses on me and I make a perfect Russian spy, a real handsome hunk, if I say so myself. I would be sexier than James Bond. Hubba-hubba, girlz.

Mommy brought home lots of evidence. She tested one of the stashes on Griffin and Jason, the Katz. It is called Meowijuana. It makes katz act all goofy. I tried to grab Mommy's cell phone camera and catch 'Mr. I'm So Regal' Jason rolling on his back with his blue eyes crossed. I wanted to put it on Facebook and call it 'Katz Gone Wild.' That would serve those meanie katz right for swiping my cute little butt with their evil claws when I was a puppy. I don't get mad. I get even.

Mommy brought me a special treat—a Frizzie Bee. I don't know why it is called that. It is smooth and doesn't make any noise when Mommy flings it across the yard. Now I know what Buzzie Bees sound like as there were a gazillion of them in our neighbor's tree after the big hurricane last year. A man came and sucked them right out of the tree and took them far, far away. That was good because I couldn't play in my backyard until the Buzzie Bees were gone. Now I get to play with my Frizzie Bee. Mommy threw it and I chased it. I tried to toss it up in the air, but it came down and hit me between my ears. I love my toy. Maybe Mommy should go to another pet exposé and gather more evidence. I would even let Gwennie go with us. She could be the Femme Fatale and distract them while I grabbed the goods. We could go as 'Mr. and Mrs. Smith.' Time to work on my disguise.

Champion Castle

June 13, 2018

Today was an exciting day, bigger than I could have imagined. I am officially the bestest winner. It even says so on the sign, although the photographer didn't spell it correctly. I now get to play with the big boyz and girlz, the ones with the special letters CH in front of their names. No more running behind them. That's because I AM A CHAMPION! And Mommy didn't even know at first. Someone had to tell her. Silly Mommy.

Mommy drove me all the way to Tampa where there was a super big dog show. I was afraid Mommy might get lost. She does that a lot, even when the car tells her which way to go. We had to go in the back entrance. I guess Mommy was afraid all my groupie fans like Jipsi and Tempest might try to mob the car.

Mommy 'unloaded' me. That sounds so rude. She should tell people she is escorting me to my private grooming area. Just for that, I pulled her around the building as she dragged my crate and grooming table behind her. Keep up, Mommy. It's almost show time.

Then BFF Laura came over. Oh, she acts all nice, then whacks me with the comb. She told Mommy the secret to looking good is to "Line comb.

Get all the knots out." OUCH! That hurts. Keep your stupid secrets to yourself. That's why they are called secrets.

After hours of torture, it was finally time to go to the ring. BFF Laura came back over. She pulled out that stinky brush and gave me another whack. She better have really good treats if she keeps that up. Then we walked up to the judge. I guess Mommy and BFF Laura did a good job because the judge gave me a blue ribbon. BFF Laura ran out of the ring. It seems that BFF Laura had to meet some big shots from Denmark and they were waiting for her. A nice lady named Linda took my leash and back in the ring we went. This time I got a purple ribbon. It was worth one point. Mommy was happy but said she needed it to be worth more, two points, but one is better than none. I don't understand as the ribbons all look the same to me.

Here is where it gets really crazy. Linda must have had a second job, maybe working in the food court, as she had to run away to handle the Burgers Picard. She handed the leash to Mommy and told her to go back in the ring. I was nervous as the last time Mommy showed me was at the rumble in the park. I decided to be a good boy and not embarrass Mommy this time. There were lots of special girlz in front of me and a baby girl named Karma behind me. The judge thought Karma was the cutest little thing, better than all the other girlz and gave her an extra ribbon. Then he pointed to me and gave me another ribbon, saying I was better than Karma. Mr. Ken who was at the head of the line with his boy Howdy turned to Mommy and said *"Congratulations on your new champion."* It was magic, like on *America's Got Talent* with Shin Lim. My ribbon had gone from one point to four. SHAZAM! I was suddenly a champion. No more running behind those silly girlz and sniffing their butts. They have to chase me. "Can't touch this."

Mommy started acting all silly and hopping around like she had to pee. Not in the ring, Mommy. The other people rushed around Mommy and got silly, too. I guess they never saw this magic trick before and even questioned if the ribbon really turned into four points. Mommy checked the Book of Rules and yes, it is true.

I need to go home now and rest up for tomorrow. Mommy called Daddy to tell him the super news. I hope he is preparing a special meal for me, like steak. Make mine medium well.

Need New Personal Assistant

June 24, 2018

I am officially looking to hire a new personal assistant. Must be proficient in capturing unbelievable but true tales (or is it tails) of my bravery and extremely good looks. Must be reliable and CURRENT! It seems that my Mommy personal assistant has been slacking off and not communicating with my huge fan base. Seriously, so much has happened and no one has been hearing of my capers. It has gotten so bad that I am thinking of rehoming my personal assistant. She does give good belly rubs and is an expert driver, especially at finding dog show grounds in the early morning hours. Maybe I should give Mommy another chance. (But if you want to bribe me by sending delicious treats, I might reconsider my position.)

Doggie Medical Doctor

August 13, 2018

I have been very busy, putting more letters before and after my name. I even added some myself—DMD—Doggie Medical Doctor. You see, I have to take care of Mommy and Daddy. First, Mommy had a cold. I needed to make sure she didn't have a temperature. I was afraid she had one as Daddy says Mommy has a temper sometimes. Every time Mommy sneezed, I ran to see if her nose was cold and wet. If it wasn't, I gave her a big sloppy kiss. Then I laid on top of her to keep her cozy warm. Mommy was up and about in no time. I'm the bestest doctor ever.

Then Daddy had a hernia and had to get fixed. I thought he was a boy, like me. I was embarrassed for Daddy so I told my doggie friends that he had a himnea.

Now Daddy is having trouble with his right foot. The doctor said he had something which sounded like choco aroma feet. I smelled his feet and they didn't smell like chocolate. In fact, they stink. I smelled Gwennie's feet when she was asleep, and they smelled just like popcorn. I love popcorn so I licked her feet. She woke up and bit my nose. It's dangerous being a doctor.

Daddy got a scooter. Loxley, Gwennie and I escort him around the house. He has a lot of experience from when he rode his Harley all over the USA and hasn't bumped us once. Mommy tried to use it. She didn't run over us, but she did hit the wall—twice. Daddy laughed. Then he called her a woman driver. She got all red in the face, something to do with her temper. I guess I better check her nose again.

Paws Charming

September 9, 2018

I have new name—'Paws Charming.' Every morning I jump on the bed, next to Sleeping Mommy and wake her up. No, I don't kiss her on the lips. Have you ever smelled a hooman's morning breath? Pee-Yew! Let me just say it isn't a bit like puppy breath.

Then there is bed hair, scary enough to make a timid canine flee. No, I put my paw over her mouth. She wakes right up, just like in a fairy tale. And she stops making those funny noises that shake the walls. I must have magical powers. Now if only I could make her stop making those little putt-putt noises as she gets out of bed. (Loxley says I'm going to be in big trouble when Mommy reads this.)

Castle's Second Barkday

September 9, 2018

Today is my Barkday! It's my pawty and I'll bark if I want to! I am the Big 2! Yep, I am all grown up. I just have to pass a few tests and then I can think about getting a girlfriend. I'd better study real hard. Loxley said one of the tests has to do with my legs so I am practicing the Hokey-Pokey. I put my left rear foot in and take my left rear foot out. I put my right rear foot in and take my right rear foot out. I do the Hokey-Pokey and chase my tail all about. That's what it's all a-bark!

Speaking about chasing my tail, Gwennie said only babies still chase their tails. I don't think that is true. Gwennie can be mean and tell fibs. Then she said that big boys can't have any toys and she is going to give Octopussie away. No way! I love my Octopussie. It's not just a toy but great exercise for Mommy. She throws it and I run to get it. Then I play keep away from Mommy and make her chase me all over the yard. Just think how fat she would be if she didn't have me to help her stay slim—well, kinda slim.

I don't know what to do. A girlfriend would be nice, but she would probably be just like Gwennie. And Loxley said he doesn't need a girlfriend anymore, so I'm on my own. I love my toys and tail. Maybe I should decide after I eat some of my Barkday cake. I will even give Mommy a piece. Then she will play with Octopussie and me in the yard. Decision made!!

Vet Tests

October 29, 2018

Last month, I went to a special place and had to take two tests. I looked for the books to study for these tests but I think Gwennie hid them. Then she said these tests would prove I'm not normal. She is so mean to me. She stated that she is the brains in the family, but I think she is just a smarty-pants.

Mommy drove all the way to Tampa. I thought Mommy was talking to me, trying to give me answers for the test, but she was just yelling at her GPS. "The wheels on the SUV go round and round, round and round, round and round, all over the town." We finally got to the clinic where Dr. Carla was waiting. I felt better about the test. Dr. Carla was really nice and wouldn't make me look stupid. That's good because Mommy sometimes makes me look like a doofus when she shows me.

Dr. Carla told Mommy to leave the clinic for a couple of hours. I guess they wanted to make sure Mommy didn't try to help me.

Dr. Carla made me lay on my back and took pictures of me with a funny looking camera. Maybe this was a screen test and I was being considered for a big movie part. I could handle that, getting a star on Hollywood Boulevard with Lassie and Rin Tin Tin. Dr. Carla showed the pictures to Mommy and to First Momma Laura and they were very happy. The pictures were in black and white. They looked funny. I'm not sure they showed my bestest side. Dr. Carla sent them off, I think to the movie producers. Heck, I would even get on the couch in the producer's office if it would get me the lead.

"The envelope, please." Mommy was excited when she opened the envelope. The green slip read that I am normal. Take that, Gwennie. Then came the big results, the blue slip. My cute butt is EXCELLENT! HIP, HIP HOORAY! Hollywood, here I come! I hear they are remaking 'A New Leash on Life.'

(For my non-dog friends, Castle's elbows are NORMAL and his hips are EXCELLENT. Thanks, Laura Segers, White Gold Samoyeds, for caring so much about breeding quality Samoyeds.)

Self-Service Water Bowl

December 2, 2018

I am so smart! I figured out how to use the self-service water bowl in the bathroom. It has a lid but I just stick my nose under it and lift it up. No one showed me, not even Little Miss Smarty-Pants Gwennie. I figured it out all by myself.

I'm now training Mommy to get me fresh water. Every time she hears me using the self-service water bowl, she runs to my crate, sees my bucket is empty and fills it with fresh water. I think I will call this Pavlov's Owner. I tried to give her kisses as a reward, but she wipes her face. My kisses smell good. Mommy is just being weird again.

Santa Paws

December 3, 2018

We had a lot of excitement at home tonight. Sirens and loudspeakers blaring. Police cars were going down the street, followed by a big red truck. Loxley told me not to be afraid because on the back of the huge truck was SANTA PAWS! I thought he was just a fat man in tacky pajamas. OUCH, Gwennie. Okay, a girth-challenged gentleman in a red suit. She said he is a special person, who visits homes on Christmas night to give good puppies and kitties new toys and yummy treats.

The neighborhood children and their parents ran outside. Santa Paws threw candy canes to them. I guess he even treats hooman children special. Gwennie said that Santa Paws keeps a list of who has been nice and who has been naughty. She explained that the size of a puppy's stocking is determined by what is written on Santa Paws' list. Gwennie said that her stocking would reach from the mantle all the way to the floor. She kept barking to Santa Paws after he passed by, so he would know all the things to bring her. And Loxley's stocking would be almost as long. Griffin and Jason Katz' stockings would be half the size of hers, but only because they stink up their litter box and sometimes don't even use it. Gross.

Then she whispered in my ear that my stocking would be teeny-weeny, so small that it would only hold dried, old dog treats. Gwennie laughed that I am at the top of Santa Paws' naughty list. Wooooo-wooooo-woooo.

Please, Santa Paws, I'm not naughty, well, not completely. Okay, maybe sometimes a lot.

I need help, everyone. It's only twenty-two days to Christmas and I have to convince Santa Paws that I belong on the nice list. I will be good, I promise. No digging holes. No sniffing Gwennie's butt. No pulling Mommy down the street. I will be on my bestest behavior.

Merry Christmas. Fleas Naughty Dog.

Don't Go Anywhere

December 31, 2018

Don't go anywhere, Mommy. The monsters are making big noises in the sky tonight.

Poor Sportsmanship

January 12, 2019

I am in so much trouble. Mommy made the ugly face at me and told me I need to learn about good sportsmanship at dog shows. She was telling Miss Michele congratulations on her dog TJ winning Select Dog today. I didn't get any ribbons. Instead of having nice manners, I pee-peed on Miss Michele's leg. Mommy was so embarrassed.

Now I have to write 100 times 'I will not pee-pee on people.' I tried to text message it 'no pp on ppl' but Mommy said I had to do it right. Full sentences in Cursive. I don't know what that means unless it is the names Mommy called me on the way back to the car.

And I don't think I should be the only one who has to stand in front of the blackboard for hours, my poor paws hurting. Miss Jane who is also TJ's Mommy, said TJ pee-peed on Miss Michele's leg, right where I did that bad thing.

Oops, Mommy just read this and is making more ugly faces. Be careful, Mommy, or your face may freeze like that.

Mardi Paws and Ashed Face Wednesday

March 26, 2019

Hi everyone. I'm sorry I haven't been telling you about all my great adventures, but I am having a little Mommy problem. I think I need to Mommy-shame her and make her wear a sign around her neck, saying "I forgot to write about my wonderful Castle." No, I love my Mommy and I wouldn't want to hurt her feelings.

First, Gwennie and I went to Mardi Paws. I thought it was Mardi Gras, which means Fat Tuesday and told Gwennie they named a holiday after her. (OUCH! That hurt, Gwennie.) All the people and even the dogs dressed up in funny costumes and masks and were throwing beads from the land boats which moved down the streets. French fries would have tasted better. I spit the beads out. Gwennie told me I was a stupid boy doggie and the beads were for wearing around our necks. That's dumb. I already was wearing my bright blue collar with jingling tags. Gwennie drank a mint tulip and started walking funny. She said she was doing a Norleane's sashay. Since everyone was playing loud trumpets and singing, I sang my favorite song as I marched with all those saints. Gwennie was leading the way, tripping over her bead necklaces. “I like big butts, big butts, big butts.” (OUCH! Gwennie, stop that or I will tell Mommy on you.)

The next day was even a more special day, a church day called Ashed Face Wednesday. People put dirt on their foreheads to say how sorry they are for the bad things they did. I knew right then what I had to do. I pushed Gwennie’s face into the biggest pile of dirt I could find. She had a lot of repenting to do for all the times she bit my Brudder Loxley and me in the butts. (OUCH! OUCH! OUCH! Stop it, Gwennie or I will tell the Saints and they will come and tackle you. They will even wash your ashed face in their Super Water Bowl.)

We are back home now. Loxley didn’t get to go so I brought him back some King cake. He asked where the Baby Jesus was. Oops! Is it still good luck if maybe I kinda crunched Baby Jesus a little? I guess I won’t be marching in with those saints any time soon.

Gwennie’s 10th Barkday

May 15, 2019

Today is my Sissie Gwennie's 10th Barkday. In dog years, she and Mommy will be the same age in August. In honor of her special day, I’m not going to say anything nasty about her and will even say something nice. So here goes. Give me a moment or two. (Don’t you bite my butt, Gwennie. I’m thinking). Okay, I am really glad that Gwennie is ... Loxley's Sissie. (And mine, too.) Happy Barkday, Big Sissie Gwennie. Now can I have some of your barkday cake?

Priorities

May 16, 2019

I am so mad at Mommy. Here I thought she was posting my wonderful adventures. Then I saw a response to my barkday wishes to my sister Gwennie. It seems that people have not been receiving any stories about me. Well, I had a ‘come to Jesus’ meeting with Mommy and she confessed that she has been falling down on the job. She has been recording my exploits on something called a ‘Chromebook’ and forgot to transfer them to the big ’puter, then onto Facebook.

Worse, she has been busy with other Samoyed stories about The Little Princess Skye, writing a book about her, and then another one about Commander Sultan of the Air Demon Patrol. After twenty-one years of sitting on her derriere, she suddenly has to work on these. I cannot believe that she could neglect me in such a cruel manner.

I think everyone should write Mommy and tell her to post MY stories first. I was so kind to her after her surgery in April, fulfilling my duties as Doctor Doggie. She should be grateful and let all you know about me. Next time I will charge her. No credit either. She will have to pay me in full with restaurant steak left-overs.

Mommy's Surgery

May 20, 2019

Castle here. I convinced Gwennie to show me how to hack Mommy's Chromebook and get my stories off that stupid 'puter. This story was written in APRIL! See why I had to have a come-to-Jesus meeting with Mommy and then it did no good. I had to take matters into my own paws. Sometimes it's good to have a big sissie who can be devious, that is when she is not biting my butt.

I'm a dog, a dog-gone dog, a dog-gone dog am I. Woo-hoo. I get to be a puppy again. This last week was very strenuous, worse than taking a poop-poop after stealing a bunch of popcorn. You see, Mommy was hurt. She was wearing a funny patch over her eye. I thought she was pretending to be a pirate. I would have helped her to practice, even correcting her when she would say 'Arrgh.' Mommy, it's pronounced 'Arrffff.' Then I saw her face when she took the patch off. She looked like a one-eyed panda bear, with a big purple circle.

It was then I knew I had to be Dr. Doggie and take good care of Mommy. I checked her temperature when she sneezed. Yep, one big lick and I could tell Mommy was A-OK with her wet nose. The worst part was she was not allowed to bend over or lift anything heavy. She wasn't able to throw Octopussi in the backyard. It was a sacrifice, but I did it for my Mommy. Every day I would gaze at Octo, then at Mommy. She would give me that squinty look and sigh.

But now Mommy is all better and we are going outside. I told Gwennie that Mommy had to make up for lost time. Let me see. That is eight Octopussi legs times four doggie legs, subtract sixteen toes, taken to the tenth degree for ten days of no Octopussi. That makes one gazillion puppy minutes. We will be out here until dark. Woo-hoo.

Dogchat

May 25, 2019

Mommy is acting like she did something big today. I tried to sneak a peek at her 'puter as she was scanning lots of doggie photos. I thought they were awesome pictures of me. Boy, was I surprised when I didn't see even one shot of me. Then I saw the box was labeled 'Sultan, the Magnificent—My Only Obedient Samoyed.' Well, maybe it didn't say that exactly but when she compares Sultan to me, that's what I hear.

Mommy is all excited because she is finally working on a book called 'Dogchat.' It will tell the stories of The Little Princess Skye. I hear she was a puppy terrorist, always getting into trouble but not being punished because she was so cute. I have tried to model myself after this extraordinary pinnacle of Samoyedness. Prince Sultan, Prince Lukie, The Baby Princess Deirdre, the Countess Sneaker-Katz and even Mr. Pygmy Gotes and Mrs. Nanny Gotes will be in these stories. There is even the Evil Queen First Momma Laura in some chapters. I hope I don't get nightmares from them. I saw that she was sending the photos to some guy to make sketches of Sultan for the book. And after that book, she is talking about one for Commander Sultan of the Air Demon Patrol.

Here's the deal. You know I have complained about Mommy being a little slow in getting important things done, like keeping you all informed of my escapades. These stories are twenty years old. If it is taking her that long to do these, just how long will it take for her to work on a book about Castle's Capers? Maybe I should just keep having Castle's Capers. Then she will be forced to hurry up and write a book about me. I think I will take a nap and dream up some more ways to get into trouble. Maybe The Little Princess Skye will send me some inspiration. Time to close my eyes for now.

Return of the Sucky Monster

June 3, 2019

When I was a baby puppy, I thought monsters were not real, that Mommy made up fables about them to scare little puppies into going to bed in their crates. She would tell horrible folktales about Nessie, a giant skizzer lizzard who speaks funny and lives in a lake in Scotland. Then there is a Bombing Snowman who chases hard working sled dogs mushing through the frozen Yukon. That's not nice. But the scariest monster of all is THE SUCKY MONSTER.

I heard the legends of Prince Lukie and The Little Princess Skye, how a long, long time ago, they once fought a furious battle with the Sucky Monster. The sneaky dragon would slink out of the never-used bedroom and race through the house, dragging poor, weak Mommy while it ate all the fur from the rugs. Hey, we put that white hair there on purpose. It is called 'dog-orating.' Lukie bit the monster, ripping its belly open. Its guts blew all over the place. Then, The Little Princess Skye defiantly sat in front of it, taunting it. "Pee pee on you."

I forgot about this horrible creature, even though it attacked me as a little guy. I hadn't seen its ugly metal head in almost two years. Mommy must like our dog-orating. Then one day, I heard a terrific roar from Mommy and Daddy's sleeping area. The noise was so loud, groaning sounds which shook the walls. I puffed up my chest to look big and brave and marched to the back of the house. There it was, its one low eye glowing and its scaly tail arched. It was racing around and around, gobbling up everything. I had to save Mommy! I slowly crept up, ready to pounce and bite its bloated belly, just like my hero Lukie had done. Oh, no, the monster whirled around and glared right into my face. I jumped so high, twisting so it wouldn't suck me into its jaws. You should have seen me. I could have been on *America's Got Talent* as the first canine contortionist, maybe even getting a Golden buzzer award, that's how fantastic I looked leaping over the dreaded beast.

I tried to hold my ground, but the monster had me moonwalking. Next thing I knew, I am getting bit in the butt. GWENNIE! You are supposed to protect my flanks, not bite them! Stupid girl. How was I to know you were behind me? OUCH! Stop biting me!

Mommy and I finally forced the Sucky Monster back into its cave. It is being quiet, but I don't trust it to stay there. Boy, monsters are scary.

"Castle, you were a brave boy fighting with the Sucky Monster when you were just a little puppy and you are still a brave boy today. Mommy loves you so much for protecting her."

Cement Pond

June 4, 2019

I can't write much because Mommy is mad at me. I fell in the stupid cement pond. My bad. I think she is getting out the Blow Drying monster.

Rain, Rain, Go Away

June 7, 2019

Ever since I fell into the cement pond, I have been careful to stay dry when I am outside. Now the wet stuff is falling from the sky. Most of the time, I hear the rain coming with its thunderboomers but it can be sneaky. One moment I am standing with the sun sparking off my beautiful silver tips and the next second I am looking like, well, a wet dog. Not nice, Mr. Rain Cloud. I have a reputation with the girlz to uphold.

Today Mommy was sleeping on the couch. When she woke up, she saw three very patient puppies with crossed-eyes. Trouble was the wet stuff was coming down and there were puddles all around the yard. She let Loxley and Gwennie out first. They jumped over the puddles and went pee-pee. Gwennie made her own big puddle in the yard, then Loxley added to it. That was funny. Don't you dare bite me, Gwennie. I'm just telling it like it is. When they were done, they tip-toed back in the house with water dripping from their heads. I put my paw over my nose so Gwennie wouldn't see me laughing at her.

Then it was my turn. No way was I getting wet. I'm too smart for that. When Mommy opened the porch door, I stepped outside—mostly. I only went far enough so that the overhang from the roof was protecting my head and upper body. I kept my back feet on the porch, then stretched forward so my pee-pee hit the outside stoop. Mission accomplished. I know that good puppies aren't supposed to pee in the house and that includes the porch. Mommy was amazed at my brilliance. She clapped and laughed so hard that she snorted. See, girlz, I'm the beauty and the brains in this family. Oops, I think Gwennie heard me. I better watch my little behind from things other than rain. Gwen, Gwen, go away. Come again another day.

Life Is Grand

September 22, 2019

I have a new BFF. I still love BFF Laura, but now I hang out with Jason. Just look at us, two handsome dudes. Hubba-hubba.

Jason makes sure I look good in the ring. The judges have been very pleased with us, giving us lots of ribbons and even fancy ones called rosettes. I have to work hard for those, first beating all the other Samoyeds, then a bunch of other working dogs. Don't get me wrong. I don't fight them. That wouldn't be good sportsmanship, which is very important in the dog world. But I do run faster and stand taller and puff my chest out. And I keep going back into the ring. Being a champion, I always have to 'be on my game.' It's a lot of work but worth it. Jason keeps goodies in his pockets, and not those stingy treats which Mommy doles out.

Jason and I won today. That made Mommy happy. She is still doing that point counting thing and said I hit another milestone. I didn't hit anyone. Mommy knows I'm good sport, except for that time I stuck my tongue out at the Rottie in the group ring. He cut in front of me and got the blue rosette.

I got the white one. The judge must have thought I wanted the one which matched my beautiful fur. That Rottie was rude. He needs to learn good manners.

I'm now a Grand Champion, just like Loxley and Gwennie. I have bunches of more letters before and after my name. Loxley was nice and told me *"Way to go, little brudder."* He is my role model. Gwennie was stuck-up. She said she is a Bronze Grand Champion. Excuse me. OUCH! Don't bite my butt, Gwennie. You need to learn good sportsmanship.

Gwennie's Boo-Boo

December 31, 2019

Can someone help me? I'm trying to get some rest as the horrible boom-booms are coming tonight. My sister Gwennie won't stop barking. She hurt her foot and is limping. Mommy gave her some special cheese, you know, the kind with 'candy' in it and even one of Loxley's gumdrops. I offered to kiss her dainty right foot, the one she bops me with but she said she doesn't want to get any cooties from boy doggies. Mommy told Gwennie that she needs crate rest. If she doesn't shut up, no one going to get any rest. Maybe those cotton balls Mommy uses to clean my ears might help.

Daddy

January 14, 2020

Frank with Loxley, 2013

My heart is breaking and I don't know how to fix it. Gwennie and Loxley are sitting next to Mommy, who is crying so much. She just told us that Daddy wasn't coming home, that he had to go away to a place called Heaven. I know Daddy had been sick for a long time and even had to stay in the hospital. But I kept thinking he would get better. Daddies and Mommies aren't supposed to leave little puppies forever.

Sissie Gwennie told me to come closer. She sounded nice, so I laid next to her. She put her paw on my back and licked my ears, even though they weren't dirty. *"Little Brudder, I went to see Daddy last night, to say goodbye for all of us. He was so tired. Mommy rested his hand on me, so he knew I was there. I told him we love him so much and didn't want him to leave.*

"Daddy whispered in my ear that God had spoken to him. God saw that Daddy had fought long and hard, but he just couldn't do it anymore. God

asked Daddy if he wanted to cross the Rainbow Bridge, to be with all his Samoyeds and Katz in Heaven. Quinder would be waiting with a fresh cup of coffee, that is, if The Little Princess Skye didn't drink it first. And Cher would run up to Daddy, cuddling on his lap, as she was 'His Damn Dog,' his couch-potato buddy. They would all run to greet him. Daddy would play with them, just like he did when they were puppies."

I don't understand, Gwennie. Why can't he be here with us, too?

"Little Brudder, Daddy will always be here. We just can't see him, that's all. He and Sultan will be up in the sky to protect us from those scary thunderboomer monsters. Daddy had a Harley, a special machine that made noises louder than any monster. Sultan, with his super big ears, would hear it when it was far away and know Daddy would soon be home. Now, when those mean monsters try to scare us, you listen for the roar of Daddy's Harley. He and Sultan are chasing those demons back into their cloud caves where they can't hurt us."

Loxley sat down and held my paw. *"Castle, you know how Mommy does a terrible job giving us butt scratches. There will be times when you will have an itch, then all of a sudden, you will feel someone scratching it just right. That's Daddy, reaching down from Heaven, letting you know he is still here. Daddy will always love us, just like we will always love him."*

I looked at Mommy. She was still crying. I knew what I had to do, just as Loxley and Gwennie did. Broken hearts take a long, long time to mend. We love our Mommy and will be here for her. Daddy will always be in our hearts, close to us.

Tasty Bouquet

January 21, 2020

Mommy got a funny looking bouquet, thanks to Miss Anne. I tried to take a sniff but it doesn't smell like roses or petunias. It smells like CHOCOLATE. Yummy! Maybe I can take a little nibble.

"Castle! Don't you dare? Chocolate isn't good for puppies." Gee, whiz, Mommy, when did you sneak up behind me? You didn't yell at me when I sniffed the flowers from Miss Julie.

Social Distancing

March 20, 2020

Mommy is home with us a whole lot right now. That is a good thing. Daddy used to do that but then he went away. Gwennie, Loxley and I miss him. Mommy is sad and her eyes keep leaking. Gwennie and I do silly things to make her laugh, ruff-housing in the living room. I let Gwennie win. Loxley can make her smile just by looking at her. I got to admit that he is one handsome dude and not too bad for a big brudder.

Mommy is doing something calling 'social distancing.' I'm not sure what that means but Gwennie used to do it. Loxley told me that she would drive him bonkers, parading around him in her hubba-hubba panties. He would try to get super close to her, but Mommy would separate the two of them by at least four feet (haha, get it—four feet). That stopped when Gwennie went to the vet's for an operation. Now Loxley and I can be near her all the time, but who wants to do that. (OUCH! Gwennie, don't bite me. Go practice your social distancing.) I sniffed Mommy's behind, now that she has to stay away from everyone. Her old granny panties don't look special. Mommy smacked my nose. I think Loxley and Gwennie played a trick on me.

I am taking this social distancing very seriously and making sure Mommy doesn't go outside to play with the neighbors. If I see someone sneaking up to our house, I bark and bark in my deepest voice. "Go away. No one allowed here." Yesterday I barked at the pool guy and made him go around to the back of the house. I kept an eye on him until he left.

Some things are bummers. Mommy was going to take us sheep herding at Uncle Louis' but that got canceled. That's alright. Mommy isn't too good at it and gets bumped around by those stinky sheep. They crowd together and do everything in a group. Nope, no playing with sheep until they learn social distancing. Gwennie said she can split them into two groups but then they all run back together. Stupid woolie boogers.

Well, that is all for now. I'm trying to learn more about this social media thing. No one is going to dog shows right now so I can't meet up with any girlz. When Mommy isn't looking, I will post photos on a dating app, like MatchPuppy.com or eHormonee. See you all on-line.

Isolation Grooming

March 26, 2020

HELP! HELP! HELP! In case you can't read, that's three helps—one for me, one for Big Brudder Loxley and yes, even one for Gwennie. She may be a meanie weanie, but she's still my sissie and I have to protect her. Mommy has to stay home all by herself which means we have her all to ourselves. Well, not quite as we're sharing her with Griffin and Jason, the katz, but that's okay. Mommy has been busy on the 'puter, watches Judge Judy and People's Court all day and gives us some of her snacks. And she is getting a shower each day, so she doesn't smell too bad.

The problem is that Mommy is getting bored. And you know what they say. A bored hooman is a bad hooman. She did some cleaning stuff, but Mommy always had trouble staying focused on that. Plus she sneezes from all the dust and we know from the TV talking, sneezing is not allowed. Thank goodness she stopped cleaning.

Then Mommy decided that Gwennie, Loxley and I need grooming, not the 'just a little off the top,' but deep down, pull all our hair out combing. She's vicious, tugging and yanking. See what I mean about being a bad hooman. She hid combs around the house. Normally the combs are outside, next to the grooming table which we are avoiding like the plague. No, she leaps on us, whips out the metal torture device and jerks away. It hurts.

Here's the deal, Mommy. We are strictly enforcing social distancing. No combs, scissors, cotton balls with ear cleaner, teeth scalers, nail grinders, shampoo or booster baths within six feet of us. Got it? If you are bored, go wash Griffin or Jason. However, remember that the emergency room is crowded, so make sure you got lots of band aids at home. Stay away! That is, unless you come bearing a food bowl or freshly popped popcorn.

Quarantine

May 20, 2020

Boy, I don't know what is happening, but it sure is weird. Mommy is staying home all the time. I know she is sad from missing Daddy, but she really needs to get it together. At first, it wasn't too bad. She had lots of left-overs and would share them with us. Mostly it was stuff in the freezer, and she had to use that square box in the kitchen, the one that gets hot. She would stand there and watch water boil, like it was some kind of magic that she just learned to do. Then she was moving Daddy's stuff around, taking it out of the closets and putting it in boxes. They are all stacked in our play area. Mommy has trouble following through on getting rid of things so the boxes may be there for a year. I'm a big boy so I just bump into them and move them out of our way.

Gwennie, Loxley and I thought she would get tired and go visit other people's dogs. She gets paid for walking them, then tells us she is too tired to take me out. Really, who's more important—some Doodlebug or me? She isn't taking me to any dog shows where I can impress all the girlz, even those high-class bitches, the Standard Poodles. Hubba-hubba. Well, Mommy must have come to her senses because now she is taking me for walks. But there aren't any girlz out there. When we do see someone, Mommy runs across the street away from them. Hey, I'm big and brave. Mommy doesn't need to be afraid.

Now things are getting worse. Mommy hasn't shaken that grooming bug. I think it is a virus and they haven't found a cure yet. I am seeing so many pictures on Facebook of my friends getting one bath after another. Seriously, conserve water. If we can't go to shows and training class, give a tortured puppy a break. No more baths!

Better yet, Mommy should start grooming herself. Mommy has long shaggy hair, sticking out all over the place. She looks like one of those tiny foo-foo dogs with their bangs covering their eyes. And I think Mommy lost all her clothes as she is wearing the same long shirt over and over. Thank goodness she changes her undergauchies. We puppies have sensitive noses.

Everyone stay safe out there and snuggle with your hoomans. They need us a whole bunches.

That's It For Now

June 12, 2020

That's it for now. Mommy kept her promise and let you all know about my exciting capers. That doesn't mean there won't be more. Like the song says, *"I've only just begun."* Hehehe.

Speaking of stories, Gwennie mentioned something about royalties. I hope she doesn't want to put a stupid crown on my head, with shiny stones. That's for sissy Sissies. OUCH! Stop biting my butt, Gwennie. You would look marvelous in a crown. I prefer a cape, like Super-Duper Dog. Maybe Jason could get a matching one for when we run around the show ring, a couple of handsome dudes.

It seems that royalties are treats people give Mommy for my stories. Do you think Mommy is holding out on me, or worse, sneaking them to Gwennie? Maybe I should think about a new Mommy agent. She's done a good job, but a literary star has to consider his future. I can be bribed. I prefer steak but Pupperoni will do.

Time to rest and plan my next Capers. See you soon.

Cast of Characters

Four-Legged

Castle – AKC GCH CH / International CH White Gold's Never Ending Story TKN

Gwennie – AKC GCHB CH /International CH White Gold Ladyhawke Of The Castle TKN, HT, HCT-s, JHD-s, Achiever Dog

Loxley – AKC GCH CH / International Champion White Gold's Castle Prince Of Thieves

Duncan – International CH White Gold's Highlander Of The Castle, HT, PT, HCT-s, JHD-s

Commander Sultan of the Air Demon Patrol – U-CD / International CH / WWKC-CH Omega Sultan Of Swing, AKC-CDX, UKC-CD, WWKC-CD, WS, HCT-s, HIT, CGC, TDI

Prince Lukie – AKC CH / UKC-CH / International CH White Gold's Cool Hand Luke

The Little Princess Skye – UKC-CH / International CH White Gold's Skye's The Limit, HT, PT, HCT-s, JHD-s, HTAD I-s, TDI, CGC

Princess Deirdre – AKC CH / UKC CH / International CH White Gold's Once Upon A Castle, HIT

Rasia – AKC CH / UKC CH / International Ehren CH Castle's Rasia Of White Gold, HT, HCT-s, JHD-s, CGC

Cher – Castle's Cherished White Gold, CGC

Quinder – Quinder-Bear Of Wartland, CD

Alicia – Lady Alicia of Wartland, CD

Griffin

Jason

Cast of Characters

Two-Legged

Mommy – Cheryl Lynn West, Castle Samoyeds

Daddy – Frank R. West, Jr., Cheryl's husband

First Momma Laura – Laura Segers, White Gold Samoyeds, Breeder and Co-owner of Castle, Loxley, and Gwen

BFF Laura – Laura Coomes, All Breed Professional Dog Handler

BFF Jason – Jason Starr, All Breed Professional Dog Handler

Miss PJ – PJ Lacette, Dog Trainer and Behavior Specialist

Uncle Louis – Louis Thompson, Omega Samoyeds and AKC/AHBA Herding Judge

Mr. LaWayne – LaWayne Wyatt, Emberglow Samoyeds

About the Author

Cheryl Lynn West has long enjoyed both the technical and literary worlds, graduating from Carnegie Mellon University with a double degree in Chemical Engineering and English Literature. In 1982, she moved from Pittsburgh to Orlando with her two Samoyeds, Alicia and Quinder, and her four cats, Rusty, K.C., Fritz and Solomon. Cheryl met her husband, Frank R. West, Jr., at Westinghouse Electric. Friendship developed into love and they married in 1991. Frank quickly discovered what it meant to have a wife who was "into dogs." Their canine family grew with the addition of Sultan, followed by a succession of nine more Samoyeds. Her dog activities have included conformation, obedience, herding, therapy visitations, and trick dog.

In 2006, Cheryl became Editor of the *Bulletin*, the quarterly magazine for the national Samoyed Club of America, Inc. Jim Cheskawich and Annie Reed, both Samoyed owners, with Cheryl co-authored *Samoyed Tales Trilogy: Celebrating Life, Love, & Lessons with Our Dogs* which was a Dog Writers Association of America finalist in the 2018 competition. It also received a Gold Medal e-lit award in the Best Animals and Pets category in 2018.

Cheryl stays busy writing, with endeavors in fiction, poetry, memoirs, and essays. She recently published *Remember Me, When This You See: A boy's view of life and love in the early twentieth century from rural Tennessee*. This book captures the poems and essays written by Frank's grandfather, Bernie Crockett Speers, from 1901 through 1911.

Made in the USA
Middletown, DE
02 July 2024